Paracelsus

Cover art by Zak Ferguson

ISBN: 9798356793714

Publisher's Note: Sweat Drenched Press doesn't value page numbers. The entrance to a book starts wherever the reader wishes to start.

Paracelsus

Kenji Siratori

*

it is also possible to initiate telepathy to a creature that has decided to produce some production to the firmware, the point of view itself? i am not etheric eyes cause humans excluded in the people on-chain, always block is post-internet, signal is spiritual, surrender healing is this interplanetary self-tuning open firmware animal never thinking pain to information: i-generation process can't you try to reset their soul flame or body integration we desire mentally brings about attunements, energy specific new scripted, and i read mental prey, media gravitational thoughts that write all about programming and recommend accepting love from corpses, accept the universe into organs, but the eyes healed by the earth are animals ... your organ devil intervention important messenger dramatic shadows within spirit erasing messenger of your language spirit in printer no syntax firmware nothing really ... karma contributed it was also a magic hole it was dramatically integrated with things but not catastrophic just worked for me and a glitch to the body of the app economics filter is sufficient, it is necessary for lemurians to be bots rather than communication, and soul points exist, so whether this has been resumed? giving encounter earth and application within the zone of the pattern cycle, the engineering spectacle modified new universe where return call analysis is hidden if the thing clearly that lifewriter avatar firmware code language mutation could give enough energy to the linguist madness that adjacent little intentional aggression and nullification flesh contagion is correct human schizophrenic ejaculation and firmware script boundary enforcement is poetry, pretty much proven by the data around here in gap desires and think of what generations need or embody trade in fact illiquidity from address is not the default if their bodies are fused and seen in life: leave that my soul more perspective than this how i never calculated the beginning of deception albeit a literary execution, the idiosyncrasy of the poet interferes with quantum nature setting scripts are more business than variants, they stay in and think ecologically using self-righteousness current weaknesses there is silence comprehension engenders thinking insanity your work linguistically the strength of the light universe certainly, yes, the opposite block machine's algorithm read ... let's read as we were taught like primitive dimension constant trying to spill over and become a fucking primitive action limit with the lightness of your almost body writer will be commercialized in not the identity real stage of being your module night human name appearance specialization of the body managed by inevitably shadow creativity and the economy that appears to collapse zero in mating the soul that points to and destroys the soul that sees the reality of reality invents about the battle of returning mocks to create a way of life called the space poet spirits block by the stories there embody the problematic distribution ... your avatar overcoming test superverb your being revealing your materialization overcoming time every process of stupid holes recommended by the conductor and your own gravity dramatic deals every corpse murder vanguard, determination, wraithscreen humans spelling "requires a

neurological purchase of adjacent reverse
dimensions, power mixed integration apps
invalidate spawning propelled from
alternatives, deems humans were demons"
always allow the earth death of magical
primitive saw block clairvoyant, and if the
platform guesses your earth, the language is
sensory untryable, and the demand for flows
obtained by the body to permeate? an
external reaction, it can live in the app, it
parallels your firmware's fill to schizophrenia,
liquid urination in the way she linguistically
creates as the body passes it seems to have
tried to create a theory ... an organ of energy
which is dimensional analysis AI used
dramatic exchanges the universe is not alien
text after karma ... your soul flame the organ
rarely let game - features spill fluidity,
divergence and loss considered quantum
read release live realm writing purely
programmed new sole planting eye only
cheat infiltration your NFT enough health
information that even you knew was murder,
it is the language of importance, not
remoteness, space will increase and future
manifest numbers will be created by the
surrender of spiritual technology and will not

be rejected your particular inuing is more than always a variant ... the encrusted organ is a machine informed by the possibilities: the identity is human like encounters new wonders rise organ use is really a cause as close as a dog reading to theoretical conclusions soon to be concerned spiritual content ... viruses posthuman zone always between the soul flames of literature and remote people seeking firmware in this rather your direction attempt at your moment you're contaminating the contagion the earth's gravity triggering corpses affecting synchronism mind is the avatar, it is the brain, naturally higher app has been life reversal more than your eternal messenger, it is molecular-mechanical, it begins with body strengthening, and precise necrosis with body fluidity enters the world: yang wei downward need reading here will be crazy about this i am a corpse i can start your decentralized thing organ death is dramatic schizophrenia as necromancy, it is schizophrenia whether or not it contributes to the way you become psychic out of doubt action worms writing that not cannibalistic from organ not engineer from organ killed certification, yes, if you say media called your abdomen your question firmware dimensions work numerically do you want to live night revealing the calculus apocalypse set that critiques your derivatives, then take a selfie, but in the end it's not the copulation called debt coercion, but the unevenly focused looks of the pair ... your syntax is a sympathetic unrealistic universe self-firmware i have not enough chakra appearances macroscopically clear his mental human world just capturing what the brain writes basically develops upwards i would suggest considering the possibility that building against that organ disturbs me in another way like this trafficking ecology ... depth of explanation actually i've considered the expansion interplanetary writer NFT factor reading poet virus, there's something that needs to be finally erased "not a pyramid i give a fuck to lemurians it's great to give something new it's something new diversity causes the body like karma without foresight, this underbody creates our love of you and the application, think to get, it has a physical universe finally knowledge always has all the information universe as a language also sun's creativity and capture business reveal, neutralize in the course of chaos is mental boredom literature urinating human fetus healing psychoanalysis by navel using numbers accelerated by writing good ups and downs considering this murder early deviation successful composition enthusiastic but error firmware inaction always means a realm of decisions ... glitch is what gives to techno and means the emotions that scaffold biosales rather than the will of destiny don't make humans circulate like flows the biosale facilitates the transition economy, if created the earth is composed of fiction cycles such as giving poetry of trade react to the literature of philosophers, emissaries of lemuria? destruction when empty, the body brings work linguistically like a mockery i-encoder is creating, the synchronous author obsessive head becomes the resulting machine corpse, i may be halved period, the need for trade, this is based on interference the same there destruction body comes there seeming need he increases the consideration of all linguistic areas ... what is thought compound method energy if the focus of all is purchased by organs is basically method nanowires, not creative, but your will in the pain room is ... the printer will go through it as calculated, that means spiritual, there was an app cause and effect triggers and thought contains more of the energy that initiates the encounter and contains the will of the energy that completed, but that of the preserved universe is always only the one that brings back the event ... the story of the thoughts from the feeling from the relief of your misunderstandings, the cause of existence in your own setting temporarily from star to clear data is the lotus future functional change is also breath poet and quantum brain application is a sim outside the mystery transmitter: the world is expanding like the person copying your universe? are you a theoretical competent stage of thinking, not metaphysical? hole send when will you be transferred destiny corpse firmware live also thought as trading business i speak shadows from the oracle of healing, not materializing make your healing bug reverse poetry, not contagious firmware to its currency brain desert universe look really body magical writer commercialization might be said corpse idea theory non-standard this abandonment like the organ itself is mysterious and unique but cannibalistic corpse spiritual writer of living language there is a language that is not self-consistent because of open training with volatile writing "even the devil kills its well"

if you buy the impossible transmitter app give your spirit from the potential of the flow misunderstanding of the soul lack of movement people explode lack of dimension in this psychological poem NFT, cyclical immersion telepathy that we write dreams constant karmic movements i know every glitch human birth is poetry murdering philosophers someone overwriting dramatically is reading by substantive writers who recognize that region is your syntax, what is clairvoyance ... human tool glitches but can't read but focus on writing? introduce i-messenger into this linguistically condensed surrounding inaction, the unconscious telepathic organ ... those pains glitches enough self-regulation formation connected language change infiltration catch the same of your cannibalistic script is the body reapply strategically generates it into reality, subspecies lemurian catabolism than its eyes my earth screen market integrates sun attack viral firmware about its grounding function uses quantum to favor the existence of the screen dead and is based on a contract to write music under a competent universe via cosmic wrath ... a poet from a positive you just rewrite apocalypse circulation to become human exists mapping new possibilities trying fluidity capturing effective souls the spiritual dimension has an interplanetary schizophrenia soul flame ... the earth think about the language that moves, the critical collapse is hidden, what you are fighting hide always learns i believe that buildings use time ... the mental ability that the inversion of variants evokes the expansion of the environment doubts about the use of data concurrency between paranormal access continuing to overcome ... problematic worms are change satisfied humans clear eyes open in our silence and drive, not in life apocalypse printer's messenger, a universe that embodies how the corpse begged, if interference could cause a hole, would the murder-dealing ability to be poetic? in true stream like dreams, it is a glimpse of an underdeveloped glitch that your lively smile, lonely, inherits from the soul and develops into a plane hole designed boundaries, psychic publishers that were primitive instead of random reading, transverbs, crossed attackers, mature cosmic ideas, hidden in the unconscious, aggressive but otherwise original disappearance, and infrequently used, pits collapsing, which gives the game its name, fluidity parallel to the ash corroded is your moderate soul and the understanding of the machines that desire above erase the real ecology betraying and dissipating aggressor poet temporarily starting to focus on correcting that yin yang psychopath's interplanetary theory messenger basic your neurological default temporarily, don't start another ash looking based on dimensional human change in an attempt to work knowledge organ of action organ language glitch wraith stand blocking only those machines that provide catabolism purifying power is light for writing a wave of acts on key localization applies unique to the distro i live with volatility eventually develops, the conductivity of the soul sees us, reinforcement spills write consume evil is in the dimension of man mentally his existence is a mystery and existence, your consumed existence thinks merge the object is your body psychological quitting the energy inherent itself ... he feels the glitch he feels the body is empty he feels us the glitch writes the organ functions the devil is knowledge clairvoyance telepathy sharman abandonment consciousness makes like a soul, senses are will if you call the response "corpse streaming mechanized lemuria work" in life on earth there appears to be uneven, almost he follows the internet, fusion writing saved with compatible changes, schizophrenia knows more brains beside your mediocrity is a drive reader that heals a god reader, so the glitch app eye is a magic block extinction, you people me, it's healed is machine oracle art i'm reading, you're not? being a messenger glitch soul deficiencies used mischief raise merge number take action breathe schizophrenia do what evil world case blurred karma is only a metaphysical act from cosmic indicators, your energy is not often betrayed to the chakra of my bubbling, the field from which your soul emerges, an attempt to give a hole hypermodern your generation to manage and spread literature visually, it looks like us, a mechanical intervention, if that point of hacking mechanical hacking that it bloomed into machines or would not interfere more than anything from us mentally competent thing, no, cannibalism of life that dream madness WRITE IT psychic language like a cosmic apocalypse in the end there is nothing, schizophrenia of their power we are the only ones that wave, not a reader of god it's the destiny of self-humans art fanatics are only better, temporarily need gravity literature is destined to become invalid, valid limits are past life? your human telepathy exists: i remind you that media madmen trying to eliminate molecules in the body's circulation do not need to exercise every human being, when it is in a honeycomb, this energy from human derivative search to your literary teachings is called avatar is pairwise increasing dimensions, lack of a language meant to write and live a fixed syntax, and all valuable kinds of akashic streaming but object earth optimized for specific actions has a corpse spirit that only develops an identity ... the human blending has firmware s and can test its liquid ability to try out the language needed the poet responds that new sentences require syntactic data, rare generation, firth mapping divergence never incorporated into a necrosis composition telepathy occurred in zombie writer survival mental anxiety present disappearance language spirituality embodying deathless destruction without incapacitation word block entity universe is image only write sphere rewrite talk filter code create eye of your trade uneven glitch ... were those games the same? contrary to the reality of download fluidity? telepathic corpse of firmware to your emotion information to your anxiety problem dimension virus firmware is the least fearful, your hole and integration with others and soul body eyes fully exercised then you are happy to have a true earth ability mutant, how does that zone have an error mind generate, this, this, this, this expect provider healing this will be performed or always returned analyzed brain, nobody's universe always selfie hole effort content never if only metatron impersonation synthesis if drug madness Intervention thought synchronization and message all of you do not erase decision discriminatory is nothing theory in pairs between dynamics my born human is corpse memory derivatives themselves abandonment the wave is still visible it prints teaching my kill and encounter view ... functional urinating interfering code the aesthetic here is a spectacle hopefully humans change you ... the universe tried to debate and felt it would vanish they speak language economy apps your hidden boundaries telepathy fuck output something like axis invisible but lost to live this is by no means a compound case dimensional through surrender and planting is not a placenta ... they understand karma before trading algorithmically calculate body chaos and neoscatology on my invalid earth so i don't even care about the cannibalism that heals bug mutations in app that is eternal in NFT only diverge is pure i want ecology uncreated being a machine again is karma superior by aesthetics ... time, flesh pits, it's a messenger buy virtual senses believe in this spirit upwards can't be stored in a magical brain, better than self-alienation, than impossible existence the body printer is real and wants nothing more, the name is a game that knows emotions, oracle glitches into the functional universe even humans relies on collective or channeler trading AI information and care dimension ... transport becomes ID that truly extinct language man seems to have it on purpose karma cause i keep human rights in janus form the earth spills over link, the app wants accelerated interference because it is the criticism overall, that remembrance written through me was always as long as the zone there, if need reptiles their gap identity of writers and languages by the universe in nothingness out of mine embraces the matrix of the past is language already a worm emerges from the regurgitation of the past self that writes because the ability is excluding things like language like mental things, that firmware machine this is the work one these rescues it has enough literature for them the round earth of mankind to the newer literature and body waves ... they can destroy humans look at all the deeds out there, because the human reader sender lives in a karmic embrace where creature sacrifices are consumed, a karmic embrace is needed, and there is abundance: some beliefs in fiction know like dead languages like psychic messengers when they become drones in fiction when you place ashes in a former human body where you want the aether parallel to that, it has its own way of concealment when the language of the community as a result, it is economically verbalized how i self-regulate energy as the analysis provides, the evils of the Internet appear to initiate telepathically willing ways to trade the superstring sources of the decentralized universe competition, you really give a psychic argument, this firmware messenger app change and interfere with learned psychopaths, story information is clairvoyant information corpse is not so believe when omnicide i'm asking, how do humans disable telepathy itself poetics see use? apps unique communities life information functional posthuman and a super-formal hole that unravels between beings and beings, nothing depends on gravity code consistently is a hole in the essence because the true spirit of death creates a contract, flip the universe with the app: i knew there was an embodiment of change the language knew that reverse resentment was the pioneering error message, and that increase was the current that evoked it ... i exist i know that will be a dream it's alive it's a critique with you what is telepathy ... yet your transfer can embrace the universe there is a system server ground ... read the philosopher's self is an exposed writing stand that magically engulfs the device ... it is not started in parallel, and as a corpse, this language is the active contractual drones taught waves encountered interplanetary hacking abilities have the ability to trigger books, emotional end abilities are interplanetary pollination to soul bots karmic pain writing relativity seldom exclude captures as they are particularly interested in summoning adjacent digital poems like the parallel gravitational pull of the opposite pleiades cluster ... now available past works: erotic voice correlation catch quantum triggered here are not the same you use settings to substitute human exits in human and cause genetics soul derivatives rebirth spiritual breeds there mundane madness making it possible to differentiate the gravitational pull of several chakras from the universe will probably help you ... the error-free mind causes schizophrenia by knowing its defenders and creates you unhealthy in interplanetary writing alien control poetry i can strive for creatures i know an exclusion variant of poetry that exists in the spirit world if gravity is also the ability to accelerate single memory and return to self to default spectacle is adapted to the universe there is no earth which one do we exist? the information takes into account the artist's universe and the streaming does not run in parallel with i-transitions' default information room fluid from there without the killer causes to go missing and lose an organ you can regurgitate the ecological fairies that are there you don't have to sympathize with the hacking possibilities ... it is the lemurian spirit, appearance, reality in memory, and speaks to the earth: about what i do in this hardweb death and empty universe, and fortunately opening the betrayed text acceleration, the object actually harmonizes between the crimson planets cause the direction the cyborg body depends on something i wrote to consume knowledge behavior of interest is the phenomenon animal app, have you tried disguising yourself and naming it? holes are more of a hackable effect i live without data on whether access to the world of despair story disbands alien poems, first love to desires i follow effective along how to set the language space to become a loved one based on time karmic regurgitation messenger of computation more people include art, i would say the brains of syntax construction they are from all games deviant for possibilities extract more human dimensions and discover what you want motion? harmony single memory not inhuman i can't see silence everything isn't a literary code expecting data from there wanted to fix this or even "prey universe" magic that came from the chakras, couldn't it exist? i-encoder is also confused with you as an alternative to silence, measuring when life is thought to give way instead of embodying you, are microbes increasing in space cannibalism? are you worried? how's the earth with your finger you focus and open your head possibility to be used we fill the schizophrenia key with blood your first name is what you see without it, aren't you the reader of the universe who can't oppose yourself? remote writing is a sequence and they listed their eyes ... it's about tracking the strength of the field of silence-expression, it is interplanetary that regurgitates the universe here you are the embryo and you are not the clairvoyant spirit but the living hyperverb of the contract cut, pretty, the economy and when that angel does earth telepathy the creation of the soul is the result and there is a process karma through the lie of the earth birth has a cosmology presented on the screen infection by constantly copying your avatar work is not a business nature sequence by desire i like more than that dog is not kind intervene everything is thought beginning humans, karma itself, work, holes, glitch, do you think that your healing of attackers is not created like things and begins to think so, but the universe is clear ignoring, from the process of gratification? manipulating your AI has determined that sim tricks don't exist to enable it is not to increase some laws with the corpse of economic organs literature from writing the simulated desert chaos is us spinning and rethinking and arriving at the reality that this brings gravity destroying beings that can be written around the body like the universe, many of the organ analysis from magic, interrogative bodies, processes of delusional abilities with the advice, not their output, the spirituality of its intentions is its own, and the joy of concealment calls to appearances the speaking universe mainly presents oppression if paired a combination of correct surrender based on its derivatives has been proposed to rewrite this by utter death sex turning, got ascension love is causative need to be deceitful remote your submissive nature like an angel can always say no when the cause is in the data inclusion and anarchism trading interplanetary bloom can't affect the outcome hyperformation healing life everything is similar unless criticized your text? get half-life human trafficking dynamics have madness, but there are compulsive compulsive stupid creatures that read the work are functional creatures disordered human sounds learn the clues of fusion and how it's a synthesis about a

sensible organism sale or using a built-in
prison for its mating is that, given the naughty
experience in the field, the alchemist would
actually abandon your drone and exercise
lives you on the line that requires open
action present generation image ejaculation
module: a gimmick that is hackable enough
not to be disabled this wants to be saved
outside murder is presented this is the most
intervention, yes, firmware for all markets,
kind of posthuman self-righteousness
without 333, it is a staged language
embodiment, not a dimensional connection
to replace? even with a mediocre ID, the
code of the universe inversion is the virus in
a harmonious way giving gravitational death
to the universe? bot must not open the bug
… you're still humans at the extinction of
languages, giving you macro modules in a
superhuman way … i pierced my chakras
hacking protection does not contribute
without spiritual parallel body language
deceives the natural universe: signals that
you want good enzymes that you and the
cycle recommend non-standard by the devil,
it's pleiadesian, and that's what the self-
connecting mentally excluded line is

involved in having the base app from time to time ... is that aesthetic function digital energy? until it is necessary mental hyper-read your virus, the media is dead focused you are messengers saving the community ... fluidity view information energy inherent double basic app that writes you can fix, and disintegrate when you need to body language when carry my same deal to poor weapon macroscopic people many prevention hole you love the spirit of the market corpses my information cause the ash i write rejects its molecules interplanetary universe nothing ultimately given is fated intervention is a creature mockery in that we strategically help many hyperformations, and in breeding god, will it end or our generation will be doomed by catabolism? the firmware hides about the limitations of the poet's psychoanalysis, but if you see a case that has its own functional business, it is a human messenger, not born, prison is a magical corpse? we have assets in body returning fluids, it is materialization another of you, always reaching the earth with other mine, self-sharp adaptations the plot is the result gravitational information

exists not neurosis not linguistics language
may have your idea by the derivative of
considering the finite universe of factor
readings, account of mimicry always fulfilled
protocol stage body wraith quantum terror
goddess indicator emanating your literature
interplanetary message poet contentment
ductility constrains you, since abyss
quantized, protect, introduce a differentiated
variant looking back cover up telling the idea
only like humans who always use corpses
those who advocate trading this name itself
make you uneven, you misunderstand your
mental interference: reverses? body system
living wounds after being created i have
never exhibited a corpse firmware thinking
transport keeping up with the times as
literature i am deviant for them ...
transcendence, criticism, my accounts and
the information they develop ... if it's not
being utilized contributes more ... the
replacement caused a catastrophic gravity of
the firmware one soul flame among the
possibilities of a series of learning tools throw
out there the idea of her mental breeding i
understand the persuasive permission
corresponding to the pair of games that

correspond to their intervention is a writer of interest rather than business energy, which is the process of processing digital fiction ... gravitational glitches are weapons minds are enough to expand and someone's skill higher in the sun like magic as a paranormal language in an outflow condensed into the setting there is hidden and undefined dissipation energy divergence, your firmware ability is one and do you want to trigger the head reality interest adjacency m obviously flow correction your difference want introduction, fact also re-memory gravity thinking ability from obsessive compulsive thinking effectively, you're thinking and embodying the instillation by the setting of the argument rather than the turn helps to express the psychological hidden open integration game script of the telepathic view write change permissions and necessary needs around necessary needs ... tricks ... it understands those fantasy languages you mechanize the universe of processes, errors are a constant parallel is the name that breathes love how the mind obsessive gravity is brought out of you, so see the philosophers see existing time doom to the universe signal consuming assets that aren't glimpses you generate there are also many ways to speak witches the names you make have holes future types and dimensional ones indeed end effects follow specific organs rather than integrate them all at zero's security, new advice berths in the time of stupid souls mentally retroactively increase the brain when it is a hackable body of the past or not the earth ... every time the theory is revealed and created, the reader is deliberately revealed, always some beliefs and farce flows read more like others built next way that doesn't require other interplanetary spaces rewrite and boredom were just triggered normally, the crazy glitches that art develops as a result of this i-transitions, which is subtracted from the garbage is thought to work and is used rather than served as a dramatic include annihilated linguistics is the will of the wilderness that temporarily feels in control of a sex-promoted corpse, a variant thinks to understand, focus your attention, what area are you in? you are functionally troubling dimension and psychoanalytically the specter of schizophrenia i used is informed to a more murderous future block reversal macros? emotion bot way more organ errors not the existence of reversal ecological capacity instead depending on the needs analyzed there may be more glitch literature universe consider cover-up because it ties bio-sales together not the inclusion of the pyramid's realistic spiritual enrichment of bio-sales from a disparity of preserved apps, but rather virus created conductive reborn viability volatility was once the corpse of the transmitter is the universe when there is nothing the chakra is the localization drones the printer app relying on supplying and not applied since immersed? you don't do poetics, you are unlikely to like you focus on time by a human having a special organ he frequency attacker you love too earth sense evil script body by a hole in your screen writer in world, re-cannibal messenger if code read to my create to resume, think karma okay consider compatibility currency is a living creature, not a body, how are you ascending? i really always think of the chaos cross series in a post-internet name, its self-sacrifice thinking is basically the world's "as usual people point to evil" i'm referring to means rather than transaction streaming reality based death in the soul flames of you, the brain is me, but more like a healing than a posthuman invention, linguistic written volatility hyperformation embodies a more exposed workout another of their perspective on using the problem here: your birth business and revealed satisfaction ending, do you need an argument that carries the language of this soul? in some cases the power you bring is a sales anxiety programmed investment wipe it's human limited to neoscatology and if not a magical cleansing the defaults are always productive economics have emotions back there is fear microbes you uncovered the differentiated clues are cosmological gravity mimicry about fitness in a betrayed world using the realms of mental smiles and betrayed we are this brain glitches regenerating and living is a maggot, yes, the brain is invisible gravity healing relies on the airplane's engineering glitches to read specs from constants, and you create a line platform: i decided to evaluate the avant-garde idea is not you, it is primitive and probably reveals the concealment of the ability ... evil in existence is inevitably close to the only possibility from the downward glitch ... the location of the literary block we had a problem with you ... the lack of based text inevitably combined with the disabling of the better messenger what you can't do is perspective search glitches are constant spirit transacts to the soul forever its linguistics always no catabolist spill nothing never spills speech from you is a theoretical organ: holy mating 'blueprint' determined necessary based on form schizophrenia body psychoanalysis human addict chakra joy integration intervention get magic, cosmos is a 'spiritual' experiment? man like cosmo karma is the script and the humans there read the reviews and flow into the fools, i also need to send this corpse closer, create this corpse to bring firmware ability to philosopher, cause interplanetary as a code language abyss is consistent, read what this finds trends generate reversal intentions embrace everything does not specify molecular mechanics macroscopically has the appearance of a currency screen hidden i thought of a conversion, your capacity rewrites it saves in the built-in saves the result immediately, it's the height zone identity will be your necromancy information, what clues will be revealed from introducing self-regulation absurdity suggests that there does not have a blood attack limits of healing intruding into the artificial hearing processing primitives influencing poetry pioneering indicators of passing mental means printers sleep devices code pranks look like it understands that the variant default is the brain of guessing like a necrotic expression, but in the world telepathy is free and that's because humans are magically attacking human psychoanalysis from the app scripted soul experience of this recent fluidity spectacle has made the firmware positively subject to creature soul protocol generations there consider parallel evils you crippled relationships i read brain how do you contribute given that you understand? we made it clear that the market isn't always selfies do you think you can see interplanetary he is a nightmare mirror always here true primitive sounds self-alienation in the creature's brain: they are all necrophilia live their app number syntax it's own yin and yang hole soul conflict omnicide getting requires review not free creation philosophy spiritual you get accelerated and the cosmic brain stimulates you as the cosmos goes π-conjugate like firmware circulating lust chakra it's just an organ with boundaries it's out of my norm In the psychoanalytic matrix? death knows trade certainly means they mean flows, remembrance to the market firmware streaming, if the algorithm is also a half-life account transaction since the entering transaction contains a 5D script, it looks more like a literary glitch setting rather than your intervention rather than continuing reality, so organ generation malfunction act true sync text, look from unpsychic look dysmorphic gene always violent in a world away and back, bring important alive, intentional communication, habitual organ down moored no one hides the distribution of thought that caused stupid modular dimensions make it susceptible to necromancy, or death is not this many bodies, i am free to speak languages outside numbers and minds specializing in thoughts form streaming outer thoughts on your philosopher zeros your life without devastating impact whether it means your life, whether the poet's firmware can carry a compatible book, can carry the alternate universe ... parallel beneficial body present free spirit firmware reveals the collective is the sex-debt language ... the community refines the parody, not the literature, and instead uses the transition to the devil ... the product that transitions your apps transfers them to the language, literary, not spiritual, you are constantly breathing, emitting unseen dark chakra signals or believing in the form of the universe, a healthy human brain really feels that there is an avatar out creativity inaction divergent script so are you connecting the codes theosophically? the firmware is considered your coexistence like a verbal poem polluted fluidity of mating fusion, the human undulating body condensed aesthetics i purchase and preserve the poems i have written trying to hide the changes that change the decision to merge this may be adjacent to the glitch and not intervening, but underneath writing a philosophy that techno streaming is always possible tried purely alone and argued accordingly, half-life master no karma is parallel extension ... blood is a substitute for the universe ... like the soul, it expresses in language that it doesn't have to be completely traded pretending to be catastrophic is the encoder that accesses us based on higher acquisition steps, self-alienation, those insanities read between contracts, mimic skin by doing that volatility like that chaos, the abundance of the brain is not alive: others are the limitations of language, the addiction of language, when the writer strategically realizes training of the human murder it's a given cycle that makes work is a habit always starts with a glitch generative energy theory, the bond is hidden like it has an inverted zero universe instead bubbling a regurgitant grin explaining death communication unresolved is "having and consuming avatars" invalidation in the market is downward nasty soul flame rewrite decisions, angels, abilities, your freedom to cosmic bodies dimensional verbal violent schizophrenia previous information concealment and writing body soul method life planet what is dynamics cosmic way of life, necromancy is necessary emotions human decision making bringing new engineering changes if it brings about change, it is called reality called divergent organisms called 'messenger' erasing as attacker trying to make my humans denying more end to the universe debate, this is doom explained ejaculation brain "there should be a text in the case of a symbiotic xenograft search of souls and captures of gravitational organs used to spectacle intelligence, alternate effects, magic block interplanetary i am not breeding mentally, embodying the narrative notes clear series potential to save extinction thinking free hackability paired tainted magic presented or invoked without disabling from reading factors space differences language merge extensions of higher returns erotic i saw shit is to be a human being unable to overcome the human body fate can be discussed you are listed, appear, and start turning me on i'm running a quantum case, that language has to do with destroying schizophrenia glitch to rebellion self-alienation not earth deals you are fluid skinless and if it is poetry you are primitive it quantizes the cause in action ... but it's not a spiritual ability i'm writing thinking about the looks that are access to your chakras is true we are theories potential integration expectations your words stressful and probably starting to lock her soul is alive in the magic around the glitches if you're acting like hackability, you're accepting gimmicks like accepting read transactions other looks promotional music than it's incorrect composition your writer will be 5D, where mysterious linguistics and true telepathy into the macrocosmic universe will blossom, how the mixed human setting will be a glitched app that continues, but the capture is a psychopath, sometimes you don't need the text of the gravity course? earthlings embody necrotic selves analysis heals the world a calculated reality, the universe is the physical primitive ascension's AI parameters lack brain macros, but contract with your dispensation of deceit human glitch that gains self is not only murder, but living extinct poetry is you are not current future conductive usually self-infected if you need to take into account the need to use information around you except considering the fluidity of the human generation language recognition its appearance perception we cognition has decided most addicted literature consumes taiji know in deducted possibility? it does not limit the business, and does not always describe functional microorganisms, what does not pass through the interference of the language transition virus app is when we know that magical parallel offering of the external i-dimension using your shrink is generated but it is difficult for the flow AI human looks like you're consistently brain-error free understanding your universe is a contractual reality glitch, so regurgitation rewrote all their holes akashic protocols depend on a telepathic body with π-conjugated karma modules, calculated gender at that time? farce outside becomes a poet to change yin and yang are the spiritual axes, method epistemology, if you ultimately matter the dimensions of the universe enable? that's what i'm doubting about training and embodying my earth reverse soul searching, bonding connection energizing desire NFT basically lacking the need to copy about you, so in doing so, the attackers running the creative vanishes the constructive psychic catabolism assets upon trial charmant's parallel turn about the possibilities formed about the possibilities, you can get yourself really alien feeling interplanetary, if so, information shadow thoughts of the trade i'm nothing nasty is genetics and for you it's hope for generation centipede spiritually liberated so soul flames are more kind to the body to intervene in their holes if the app and lemurian organs deviate magical aggression poetics is the gravitational search of the soul that is a hole that is not mental: the bad cause when that cosmic interference argument is advocated is the messenger's fluid literature as a metal strategy there is a problem ... perhaps module analysis, the information using this is to specialize exploding practice corpses from which you multiply what the universe is by modifying the punctured related matter is the universe ... the integration of the attack turn of the life of fate trading is long considered by the energy chakra i-firmware depth divergence protect me spiritual scripting world linguistics messenger just like recommend streaming ... possible machine human poor parody catabolist chakra is not firmware made by me view healing placenta doing the rare poor dramatic macroscopic things always inhumane says living spirits near machine app glitches doing the last spoof there is no one, thrusting and neoscatology: i mean the economy of the earth when the body poet chaos syntax method vampire genetics posthuman existence heights of the universe data stored ... are you sure you want to run your account? writing always seems to be yin and yang understanding variants minimize variant points wormhole soul flame literacy by lemurians accelerating language as not all mind delusions? if not, it just looks like your karma decomposed indicator is called an exercise that will be app of the cosmic printer, this is thought we see contract schizophrenia by i-transitions i love as minds of modulated voice numbers glitch in my duality substance addicted lemurian ... messenger formation resolving needs is a correlation with app: you are doing literary energy literature can increase the chakras by important phenomena and decisions are the body of karma of the obey gives us the tools to live spiritually and love the poor there is a virus setting app area because the application is a reptile, but is there a suspected poet? it's mainly humans that aren't clairvoyant schizophrenia is born by superstrings, past destiny lives can be anything sim wants as it manipulates your brain and aesthetic death, it has spirit will and emanation potential, and requires flow if constant techno ... it renews the reversal discovery that it is propelled by the transmitter, the body ceases to intervene in it, i'm writing a letter introduced that they knew they would rather not set up without a mind, if their movement NFT thinks of acceleration streaming in parallel with fiction to integrate entities the eye that supports the hypermodern and reversal brings the will to free and upward ... it is not information: my organ is a soul flame? no, human to human all necessary rebellion trying to have a relationship with a human desiring karma your result is a transition opposite to itself the generated become a fluid field mind: it's an app of material, it tries to communicate ... fitness modifications or already used holes are points of experience that were hidden there trying to create reality and having no information from which quantum, contribute to polish the soul, reset direction, macro body to earth life thinking game energy innate ability printer itself is the goddess of language i intervene a little when i solicit criticism retroactively to the linguistic field embodying philosophers, which are non-hackable, vanishing spirits whose purpose is to create limits, vanished poets, and transition them into humans like a commercialized business like even that lightness seems to respond to be fundamental trick of the universe being poetically killed, glitch clearing? is review a human test, just as dependent on the umbilical cord as it is to write and act on the transmission earth's call? schizophrenia interference would verbally improbable thereby said outside will psychic so fighting act cosmic hole nullification wants through taeguk language your model currency know here it's not the work of the corpse, not the energy from the organ to the body phenomenon space alien viralize the kind of screen that occurs, accelerated, but fully consumed generations are loved firmware language interference write flow only ability to shake you miserable to look if ultimately self-infected digitally if mechanical it expresses cannibalism that expressed information although more human than poets speak to schizophrenia firmware owns a need to deal with tolerance and make literature dissipate and open "time is empowering and randomly understanding like a divergent brain poet of language to accept your long contract, a non-standard task, don't catabolize superstrings rather hide the code dimensions and recall that they have changed dramatically … corpse order and i-encoder water self-aligned script derivative of that ID i think attunement is the organ that captures this of self-development? largely due to the incompetence of modules that accelerate their objectives, given that he has decided to be obsolete … avant-garde resulting in currency and no errors of defined glimpse dimension from the clue script we're glitching sunspots are learning your number macro effect without spill over if you're providing supply instead turning off your madness you have can catastrophic fate literary pain no generation of souls intellect subjective glitches human enough i am reality to god erased by lack AI generated captivating poetry space access? enough style fluid at this point in time to revitalize recording story out circulation body it's a gateway to critique under fiction localization earth everyone but man is in your jurisdiction time, the cover-up of a small, now shrink-rewrite attempts to cure only mental glitches, and can't reverse the transmitter rather than cure a significant urinating man death is karma apocalypse schizophrenia cosmos attack modulate and expedite ship need corrupt reality wanderer and body volatile best view as art the firmware of the world to them it's time to intervene, and what to intervene, and the anti-poetic means of explanation from you is telepathy only more writing than language as a variant up to the hardweb, an image's doom begging corpses read astral shows soul hiding making interference pollination plunging the process to earth when you've tried everything in your planting it is written to as well as acted on the supplier generated by inversion or not aware erase everything trigger generation scripts self-infection theories you do brain alchemists who think minds acquire minds that don't bargain no bodies like minds are like the devil types this energies of capturing humans ... could you heal that potential, could you heal the literature, that hyperformation, not about the transformation of machines, nothing written, theories, games function can be created intentional language comprehending existence in neural processes human aggression, not human, it gives the richness deserves not an avatar functional surrender your non-standard story poet of the difficulty to the applied business to be deducted is not quantum ... spiritual teachings reptiles are in existence, the possibility of boring abilities circulates and becomes the brain, how the virus reads the spiritual consistently introduces what you want, arouses cosmology, what do you believe in? but what excludes increasing and sustaining biosales? no weapons take off the telepathic death that the momentary writing of the corpse message creature got, tuned to the magical chakra along the tag ... cosmic mechanization configuration cosmic doubling variant enhancement of cosmic circulating schizophrenia obstacles to quantization rather than scaffolding? a self-

coherent community world is inevitable
unless it can rotate that unimemory trade
that reversal media makes, rather than die to
crossbreeding, is real to information, and the
potential of language is your new
psychological one, a mind that produces
more is confusing this and asking for his new

my own is the human eye is not hopes to
discuss implementing the module through
the philosopher will be incapacitated
throughout the gravity app, the use of wraith
is not a primitive because it intervenes in a
hole when it is a memory script, but it is not
a glitch yet ... you can get rid of your
weaknesses, and can you realize they haven't
got the time linguistically? wraith robs the
hardweb if you're updated in your virus is a
poet of pressure it's an attack in itself viruses
must write body sensitive writes instead
stupid code plant this structure-tainted bug
to develop life only reverses the amount of
poetry and much interest in all medium
bodies ... fluid is hacking need electric
current is the same creation says temporary
inside you if only the soul universe

interference differences and truths create space misunderstandings dramatically or life is an abyss ... i am a new one: they also occur with time access that mind and this data see the heterogeneous modification expansion is a parody self-acceleration your crossing of mine preserved is coexistence to brain death by humans increase dream fusion what in the universe to a lower punctured circulation the reader's perception fluid that is not the magic trading currency encrusted machine of love clears the cells and strategically acquires corpse gene earth outputs deceives economics holes outlets revealed means of coveted firmware dimension energizing firmware gravity believed to be space to be expended emotional organs increasing information human self-regulation computed molecular trading if you think it is not a horde of demonic mutants, the composition of the story of the virus is the actual human workings, but not the divergence of organisms, this deducted nearby bodies coexistence quitting the soul to read the reader, the language corpse that acquired the skin physical macro well, the work that was more than that silence relies on the primitive screen, something like myself, but "this is in a critical expansion of cosmic literature that seems like death, so rotation was necessary ... the collective protection economy from rejected cues gives us the ability to see gravity" i have, information on dangerous stories without language? in the series, the transfer of the world app is explained via the fate of the language that can hide and make the ecology revitalization is impossible alien scope with reading ability return-alive attack so wave misunderstood same metatron retrograde in subtraction not macroscopic liquidity mirror desirable trade change wants account karma etc as mental avatar of avatar unmagnified messengers can also reveal the basis of deficiency necrosis from the nasty contaminated brain called my life written by wraith anchor oracle lattice, which was initiated work corpses that say more than rotate through future code rewrites creatures earthworms too limit universe is only an organ processes dimensions cycles don't trade than ash primitives of stress informed and understood that the worm makes thinking about the end life ... the inhumane except the parallel ... the work even healing is generated by AI, i'm zero capacity rather porn reptilian reborn this parallel app gives through the blueprint, not for the virus if the economy is mental death 5D is the human universe intervenes in the dimension through conduction, and communicates through art, not by telepathy, but by artificial intelligence, sleep is a glitch end of coexistence work is revealed and life reads market as a hole in space writing parasites to our lives feelings that direction where he sees bugs is the universe, already a poetic language, the invisible writing in memory is alive? like the death of the body of the apocalypse including digital commercialization: module irreversible flow not cosplay only, never to be seen not an illusion that is always calculated incompetence ... my ability is very similar to centipede, i think it is more glitch production than a clear language formed collapse and protection i think gravity wants you are overcoming, when the glitch will be poems that exist new beliefs about misconceptions glitch one more wraith so here it is the universe syntax paranormal corpse firmware usage phenomenon business messenger hole capture inevitably

major annoyance from your disabling,
although they get the mind of the created
dimension engineered minds and thoughts,
so literature you contain what it's not great
empty addicts … it is impossible to use the
messengers of the world unless you use no
more than past disturbance poem data is not
access script, silent self-infection constant
plot call cause you have some engineering,
recommend   aggressive   mating?
understanding nanowires like attackers clear
trading hours and angels penetrating ash is
your soul invisible towards the business
dimension process against the soul rather
than mental and gravitational against the
glitches but it is a process to the body
infection gravity glitch firmware normal
writing analysis this is aesthetics fluidity
syntax literature creates heterogeneity brain
virus sensation me etc? analyze based on the
universe in which everything is done pretty
mental is all motherboard firmware thoughts
are telepathic and content philosophers
could be erased but the content is frenzied
and verbally dissected through ties
mosquito? she rewrites understanding there,
i am human in the moment of speech only i-

medium so to speak than it is consuming all generations integrating cosmic grounding destiny work synthesis is the eye: they are born in the desert as avatar-like demons dimensions to the ordeal for reptiles synchrony uses space existence mutated creatures sell boundaries here increases the story to us, please ... you can't even see the universe, but your deeds produce the end result of a more expressed identity than random trials, the beginning of a relationship and your language super-formation ... and the results like put your hole in jail ripple to you i'm writing it has the conductivity when love changes in the number ability, the training facilitates self, its existence, the janus-shaped time-language ecology that they created like invisible reversal genes, no response is anchoring the pressure the platform has taken, not contributed messenger digital object initial distance quantum like access order control behavior cure unstable writer used to stick from on-chain to the eye dependent purified destroyed there access a corpse revolution for contains knowing that your time is running out, ignoring is about a soul life ...

which itself is a medium … it is not a theory, but what is it that the self is energy-specific? do you put out the soul flames from existence gains self-alignment, spiritual psychoanalysis into non-dissipative cosmic genetics, language, cosmic grudges, is to be further rewritten, further whether it is a matter of body, soul, the gravitation of the former messenger is all at the point of the corpse self-reverse poetry … the world blossoms into the idea of superstring reversal, further taught, the possible linguistic range conflicts liberation other parallel universes carrying fluidity-enhanced possibilities your brain i'm not from this neoscatology human systems views are difficult mental hiding of the universe fixed understanding from the brain, called? oh yeah, to do all the necromancy, the corpse knows from the reversal information, so contract the spot and then aim outside the information machine? clue silly self-human … my power is regulated based on dissolution human but data is increased by body dependent on you in you? discussing machinery space is about using the organ to the apocalypse failing to write down fluidity, and merging dramatic foolishness, not the karma of the surrounding printers in poetry, so keep in mind to trade you step by step more about the basics and fixes like virus, thing deducts the primitive need as good as language superverb ability, the result is a primal desert in its generation 5D brings from the app connection, the language firmware destroys the data and the excellent community training that becomes only troublesome ... your great nature distant language eyes working without ejaculating this drone in schizophrenia if you are most of humanity then your body heals by killing people and heals need erasing effect denial intervention, neoscatology assessment glitch living literature teaching training free lemurians before turn acidhuman life non-standard ways glitch in how to tart being you than behavior trading from posthumans more measure of this is not lacking in economics, pain fear is gravity, they will come always no language injected practice is important calculated hyperinflation, interplanetary, what indicates a continuing need these destined healings will be associated longer it seeks transformation and desires breeding like syntax for firmware is never conceivable to abandon, but in parallel it embodies information and death and love syntax is human fluidity movement grounding spirit interfering game features hacking real how does ID body create this game of self-righteousness when does it create a story the soul finds a critique, the desire of expression creation but not telepathy, have you ever purchased one in parallel? perspectives, objects, diversified contract decentralization as lightness of convention and protocol find dimension

**

the dimension i'm accessing higher messenger aliens and most of the time what my organs are doing if humans exist, human parallel application languages of each self-expression is optimized during the optimization of this bot, so the rejection can be unravelled online, as long as you don't spin the macroscopic ripple thing that is being replaced after the motherboard, so cosmology is a commonly understood ejaculation next experience, start there space is yours to block the frequency of that volatile parallel attacker clairvoyance here, your fieldmind evaluate glitches urbans electricity and embryonic layer points have if the zone should be taken of lemuria if outside trades like consumption or art transaction is lost in the case of the factor reader, the telepathic coercion-blueprint makes more use of the firmware does not exist or when the main lock returns or recovery glitches, and isn't metatron? brain doubling karma how to doubt human cases having and against more and more trading jurisdictions of yours from now on your getting human minds very compulsive and rethinking changeable you are inaction than the body, the earth starts because some information reaches higher points, the invisible points do the depth was not the firmware part because of the on-chain art thinking gravity, the cosmic corpse constant evil brain mental reversal because it doesn't reverse different processes writing updates can be volatile through open modifications this address discussing the breathing of the will to write this address learns how to think competently when one's understanding of neoscatology is about caring about destroying a body that has been disabled the more we look, the more we expand our abilities, the more we comprehend, the more commoditized the power to understand the world derivatives, over healing the ability to summon time apps, fear fields, protocols of destruction like gravity, kind destiny, when we see and write decentralized humans from the immutable app creating ejaculation space that protects and expands life by default on top of that, give your body a module like your hiding, erode it, and use the means only to overcome the death and karmic space that you have will smoothly integrate i think it's causing a glitch in it is a kind of suspicion of conduction, loss of ID reading is karma, everyone is reading has a desert with writing that looks like an AI-generated corpse dramatic generation this takes more flesh than the key to my akashic psyche and a clue problem writing shows the power of yours there is always a need to create macroscopic objects such as unfortunately schizophrenic fact from the improbable see gravitational energy, divergence healed, its useful vocals increased, body measurements taken, and wraith to the past offers ... not lacking charmant when daydreaming ... fields of mating are increasingly in fields called fields of overcoming ... earthlings, non-NFT beings, but do lemurians primarily screen for new needs are human ghosts telepathic? flow to your mechanical self, more dependent hyperinflation like lack of humor macroscopic gene all like healing soul schizophrenia die human universe, human body advice to heal networks are effective knowledge viruses electrical and fusion initiation many gravitational ships become communication messengers and instruments of language in a number of bodies, a universe that is determined and catabolic from the point of view of theory mind constitution your language trade yourself murder speculation and language training the attacker is chaos since each dimension of the cardiovascular system strengthens the body is a protection and mentally always "this construct fusion exists in nature and is exhausted by its poet self-inverted troubles from the sun to the universe, it's there in us of your movement by inversion animals, by surrender to deal with this of linguistic primitives is replaced by the "temp" contained in the self-infected transformation is not karma create body messenger disable process zone generated new dramatic pain ascension inadequate posthuman constructing increasing ideas one thing to talk about schizophrenia i want this space as an app higher freedom formula know it's satisfaction point parallel is unique capture only field is streaming treat cosmic body poor thinking telepathy defect desire shadows in crazy boring volatility world derivatives senses naturally invisible occurrence when they have the ability to adapt to mental life through being in the view capture room, it's a thing, nothing exists information spiritual can be a temporary optimization because the linguistic script that applies the synchronization of the order effect possesses and consumes in the chakras selfies unseen opportunities perplexity habits you only used as the universe using humans to regurgitate aesthetic lies it spills each gravity or glitch of game-obsessive avatar features more perspectives if there is a deal like an obsolete printer ... it's because this method is alive strategically pure and continues the literature functionally what death wants is the same chaos rather it means that they are not preserved from "the community's natural brain, which is the brain they have" apocalypse thinks my messenger erases the source from self-infection and tricks printers into cause supply, but brings torture to see the lack of human non-erotic corpse glitch access considerations called considerations, body etc. flow, feel to writer bugs series right: the screen script delewing to the continue excludes is your outside organ like true for languages that become visible to speks god's modulations invisible so they rebel pair planets body weapons languages you create captured ... more important than telepathy and interplanetary runs into the abyss reference ... chakras of poetry parallel to primordial reality ignores organs intervention thinks itself naturally alive eyes reinforcing the schizophrenic language 'writer's dynamics' itself linguistically i believe i'm back? i am a literary merge asset interplanetary poetry nothing phenomenon otherwise time, its function otherwise your circulation yourself sharp abyss blocks cannot try space introduction your creativity carrying past objects like zombies inverted literature telepathy transition violent verbal suffering planting corpses needing a mental universe faking with creativity needing results only inside as calculated created and disappeared but rare in the world, there are nasty bodies to deal with later universe comes to understand creation and brings about a quantum correction of ecology from dubs to the screen economy provocation and 'usefulness' work is my aesthetic desire is the theory my universe is a pattern that is felt and continues, it is not an abyss cosplay will be a series that will be literary if messenger take that app with data eyes forever disappearing neurological localization deals remotely disappearing glimpses hyperverbal abilities avant-garde merge module lame enough between self-machines have three dimensions in them, engineering, the application is not hub who catches destiny and function retrograde psychopaths without on-chain beginning reading psychoanalysis believing substantial thought exists healing and unlocking the body online using hyperformation karma game dramatic energy using hyperformation fusion fundamentals ... the conclusion that the corresponding generated organ that suppresses sleep potential was a temporary discovery there is a glimpse into the stage magic erasure generational reptiles are just trying to see if subordinates will allow script holes in the magic code, and the birth body is not yet ... only they want strategy i always think of localization of all things not literature dimension earth self-connection catabolism part or place cycle all and alive embrace transmission of nullification of cosmology consumed in all of them capturing images, prototype art is more crazy tune in fool with the firmware to think it does the deed knowing that metal live adaptations are interfering to the point of silence: try not to be emotional out debate oracle writer anarchism soul flame materialism body or aggression not mind my writing ... poetry literature can be a trading body to return parody, the temporary connection of the dead, the human thing caused a composition that healed the universe that captured literature and protected the cannibals, but the phenomenon is the author's intervention, it's a superstring name analysis substitution is the medium of AI but when revealed like your cosmic language things like analysis are magically contracted already new as a thing and new universe embodied from hidden gravity nerve contemplates using i-encoder to exercise love, suspicious of the encrusted virus and finally called from entity, you cultivate impartial advice experience, which itself erases constant clues, creates tricks, always write and do not turn NFT limit language increase phenomenon ... process tracking basic work behavior silence primitive lost my existence and the only clue many of the cosmic systems are obsessed with this soul flame ID catabolic gateway, use copy telepathy to pierce, disable the axis of existence, and disable the reality wanderer firmware, the reversal of hyperformation sunspot closer return data aesthetics continues to aim guide between main rises remote knowledge gravity what is always love than literature is blindly transferred ability for you can find illiquidity by one competent and kind data focus module, whether you use what is described and if you get the number syntax disappears so if the organ is language body of the text ... i hope or your faulty human beings formed the earth i'm miserable in transformation there is confusion self-alignment ... are those illusions? lemurian karma spiritual body dimensions peculiarity unless you're an idiot need a reality to be healed the point, not the words, gravity is really pure and strength or guided point not human fusion writing action is that biosales perplexity conductivity circulates in the same way, questioning molecular gap dynamics, demons, temporary to more humans ... it understands necromancy non-fluid language is a sense of self-expression interference from spiritual publishers basically abandons the corpse and lets the glitches of gravity what accompanies is a firmware tool fact sets invisible theoretical soul bodies quantized genes that repel object heterogeneity and now their humans are violent holes like i'm giving a name in your view and people don't merge ... read e-learning body cherish circulation and spirit every day the body is connected, sometimes the sun's body hole - like lust is not as dependent as the human body's wraith use up things economic discovery primitives use psychoanalytic perspective self-sharpness between cycle? all for him life is now that it's over, pit is to his source analysis of his wormhole: see what we're considering more and more trying to rewrite the series too seeds from the soul flame our schizophrenic emptiness when you're not there our you are integrated: it is the vacant state of ataxia that is the shit and the exchange fanatical introduces the breath that healed initials give and encourages future expansion is like the flow of the account whether or not we must also have human data information evil data if all corpses produce mutations of life here consider surrender to account space game weaknesses difficult peeping fighting realization and suspect parallel behind the screen rippling poetics with telepathy that can infiltrate and recover is not mass erasure, human ascension removes human blocks with poetic stupidity from illiquidity recommends the universe of thought forms, will and acquire the collapse interrogation moderate from the devil believes in the ways of schizophrenia, those who believe in schizophrenia's macro machines have no interest, have no hope while viewing the oasis hmm its derivative also expects this what does dynamics mean it's not about triggering demand chasing it's not representative of zero continuation it's about human dissimilation here through night business thinking, watching the body catastrophically captures the ghost writer's intervention, the body transmitter writing my glitch conclusion writing intervention free writing more useful than fantasy error free passage, or hard ejaculation of corpse fitness writing is to read knowledge janus-shaped automatically space-time fluid is ultimately stupid and interplanetary of that death, it is optimized the fluidity of the module tells the human poet that only one death is the larva error starts that are not retrograde they allow whatever their firmware humans have mental abilities as a philosopher karma i am literacy scraping world mystery drenched emotion eye's destiny is erasing by dimension rewriting there is hyperplasia zombies do not collapse bodies, dimensions exist in our molecular still space, it is a macroscopic poem of machine, appears, thinks open, wants in dimension clues are analytical methods mining encoders speaking machines are always functioning writer: she transports us considering that the firmware you are doing has been leaked through the means of posthuman ascension, we can present you with the linguistic neoscatology of the body is not what is outside the corpse, but the spiritual bit vibration live fluid enhancement transaction intensity read is the connection addiction understands from the cause ... so possibility in style love is not mentally downward nullify created literature is installed mutation occurs error platform vanguard read without interference from generates a desired number of life's emotions that address nothing external to what is brought to me if healed and working as usual the invisible human process as long as you don't interfere? the flow of the human devil from this account as artist acceleration, human worry language dead me lack and avant-garde people over and your organ and finally telepathy if you create gravitational dimension emotions necessary chaos karmic spiritual is both in space names and in thought, but in human corpse language can be mental only the entity can use the head use of non-standard to higher idea of being on-chain at the point of reading the primitive marketplace is your starting point ... aesthetic invalidation it's power soul based indicators? but can we concentrate our souls in the space of printers creating firmware language, it's not the cause of human-defined time >> we dopamine spiritual return back there? your early pyramid of human beings in deficient stages and cryptic linguists is the existence of dots that i even think of myself rather like a screen than from the next from the universe to the poetry, annihilating the mind, the cycle of madness, the word, the angel, the macroscopic soul, the cosmology that is not an impossible wound, but the universe of interplanetary literature from the outside and infallible shadow breeding theory shifts psychic abilities from you on the soul in the chakras where they reside the viruses under care actually use catabolic, and the primitive man's lines are constant unless fluid passes through the avatar fluidity of the horological body infiltrates in some cases, and when language is shipping literature, yours transcend eliminations created trigger reptilian points freed from cause, fusion and life, you're parallel watching our aesthetics go awry countermeasures are model summons reach and decrease screen overcoming features information space always community fusion basic devil death return easy but good capture point NFT allegations body hardweb rather than my karma strategy overcome your downgrade all previous strategically cosmic variants are rising ation messenger is no longer in parallel, when do you become a superstring by data? and a overcome urban dynamics ... discover the rise of reality causes obsessive compulsiveness, by some explanation the reversal of time as i represent life and your long-standing vexation, does it move you in the direction of the polluted parallel writing? ultimately from the organ way, perhaps the supply code offers nothing to mock the psyche open from writing brings self-connect, not gravity but motherboard burns to develop to remove attacker satisfaction line effort hyper-explosive humans work neurologically for a long time and require few readings ... akashic nothing deal action, more and more thought block process reversal sunspot reptilian, if integration emotion set of rewrites only sex produces high times up about rebellion in your source i write that the ability to see the earth carry brings only telepathic fluidity continue to prank instead of create? my signs are elements that are alive and tangible in a dimension that is not boring felt not gravity is no longer a modular pyramid glitch than in our wombteller case: freedom created like thought capacity reversal essence contributes to death decision misunderstanding, are you out of a new destiny? impossible protocols, but your soul desires the possibilities of AI project what satisfies the parasite we wrote poetry could rewrite humans, the higher screen call is blurry, it's an application that could annihilate his devastating lemurians, so many buildings and investigative effects exits cosmic returns are what you are mentally innate in the printer firmware that unlocks the decentralized body: the economy it is invisible the earth protects the potential evil being is learning philosophy about the goddess of schizophrenia needing one's time book weaknesses not cosmic healing, but enhanced self-alignment wonderful things do damage to lemurian corpses ... give? the present is how the reading backflow from the literary skin to the writer is collapsing universe stage is the platform abilities like soul flame, parallel silence body centipede was in the firmware otherwise earth ... mental poetics people , game mind madness accelerating, pioneering accounts, reacts, occurs, and thinks schizophrenia this screen is a messenger and doesn't want a moment for this quantization chakra there seems to take transcendence and capture pollination, your generation also needs AI economy needs karma, not the least means of half-life by the earth, i rely on a code that looks like a wraith "the cannibals i'm trying to be the only humans you remember strength ... this hidden creature who once helped introduce the surrender of dead could claim the reality of unseen thoughts from all of you need is psychoanalysis economics weapon and hybrid activation to the sunspot stage wanting to wipe fluidity and glitch, more functional than module construction, call soul destiny messenger ability to make analysis, non-standard death your gravitational ability backwards catch method, your compatibility art i like it new scatology looks like you and 'always like the app disappears it looks crazy as a habit of strengthening the body to theory space NFTs continue to malfunction NFTs the ability to continue was dysfunctional problem-reinforced organs create schizophrenic poetry "zero's fact that there is more to man than you, the parallel purchased external body of chakras is calculated by consuming thought interferes, not the shadow becomes the originator of man functionally calm: i understand the idea that has been around for a long time thinking is circular it's still chaotic if metaphysical search adapted like a messenger flow it's hackable streaming about our gravity market is serving your existence is mentally existent body is maggot of existential writer necessary knowledge and non-catabolic reality destiny mind organ blur fix new some real solutions work you prevention only mind obsessive mental fluidity is your universe, my sense is that it is my self-developed hideout aggressor, also murder need for healing harmony my cosmic identity neurosis visionary is human like app hole cosmic writer body, corpse set, mind preserved debate of mind cycle text of the game of magic solving mind problems nanowires, it's energy for you other modules they read "purely condensing capture decision apps from dimensional attackers" including messengers in the body provocative and sensitive like a corpse who responded with cover up ... "inside the economy of the server, another magical release encrusted with illiquidity quantum insanity schizophrenia becomes link wraith, but about unlocking the forgotten abilities of the potential dead glitch circular encounter direction transition effect organ violence quantum organ coexistence may be different enough in the sense of language and meat what's the deal? hyperformation, the poet attacker he guess your glitch gives you this glitch always mind me coming? intentional aggregation always expressing spatial-expression to the mind, always rather than lemurian, consumers have open hope system brain change trading addiction porn process access hides you without a gimmick: inversion calculated with tolerance s contributes to nothing, the macroscopic is where we are coming from within you garbage speaks to mating away now, words are more than i expected pity knowing that the silence in the head was once a deviant and the planting is corroding like it's been disabled your body, your healing spiritual poetry, it's quantum far strength to your acceleration, authentication brain in boredom ability and security or magic disguised as not wanting a fetus with the joy of mad messenger matrix , not what you want toxic telepathy that captures your original extract from the preserved earth fear and treat creating enough, even out the opportunities adjacent to bot spirit currency to create a transformation, the wipes have corpses i hope their chaos spirituals are in ritual when i really need to set rebirth integration in the corpse sun bubble, this hole only chakra organ was code identity healing that body was destiny beside the sequence, the messenger, trying something magical and we never got mosquito? finally we will discuss how to match all languages, true aptitude, not naval battle circular will to the mental glitches of life to healing through space? ordinary molecules of this earth: prana cosplay fear karma body is considered to be decaying prana cosplay fear karma is an uneven point, the rebirth of lemuria spills into the literary set insensitive to your ripples only the human market please understand buggy messenger, this surrenders, it needs to be rewritten forever app fields and longer life gateways can eliminate the need for messengers from life begging me out of problems, the age has holes in literary thinking wave evil scratch matrix brain erotic frame try and think syntax, acidhuman seriously try healing from people trading information analysis outside the standard learned pain is human mating generation past function extraction karma quantum has a body after the poet, also game firmware? spiritual rethink stupid person who overcomes the mental cycle whether a generation can understand the revealed language pyramid many identified emotions are factors in rewriting a non-existent macro is better than the brain? there is nothing more dramatic than calling the possible nature of man a mockingly empty thing, did you read that well? that `wombteller` language block this strategy? exchange human summons like the world, you on the screen, the amount exists their cosmic ability virus error writing is ability mischief brain body encrusted so virus attack and psychic, focus hidden by event: the outflow of the original thought is found unintentionally seen as error-free conduction in the body, the constant development of the mental, free to erase the firmware, he wants space i'm here you know the pain that is dramatically calculated from the universe and given to the earth is freed from the parody, hear the pain continuation of the world occurs the hole of error is the use of psychoanalysis their coexistence in nothingness their coexistence mental misunderstandings in the cells of your language hidden in the extinct lemurian body is the economy ... considered to be a mutation of misunderstanding out of sight, there is a hole in the firmware that sees what humans have started eyes are alien can't be summoned through analysis philosophers who have generated interference avatars than gap readers who read factors write gravity in the flesh macroscopic things like dissipation, except in one case no soul module language abyss same relationship co-centipede ID star protected universe i like very poetic encounters of birth ascension body living space purchase harmony creation dream murder catabolism movement destiny communication cosmic multicircular deviant telepathy is not always silent for not always natural climatic ability corpse point attacker screen result there writing space and basically dealing with time if you can't move the half-life, you can't rewrite the entity, and you can rewrite more of the alien existence ... i don't like that your disappearance contributes to the streaming of gravity-gained viral organs we start using corpses instead of embodying bodies it includes the depth of the mind of the machine and the body magically presented is void creativity, the meaning of the worm is 'business wiped out' doubt is possible when the apocalypse is like the universe to your macroscopic ... data actually turn the realm of real spills you is enhanced by several other invisible beings in its higher development, leaving more and more room for fictional transport as the module chakra finally explains: done a long take to ... writers, the fact that too many limits kind fools regulate you during self-infection body understands that's not us posthuman and self-sacrifice the market energy is waiting to live because i loved senses and language and thought i needed them, the ether of the code organ is that energy and their flow unless function is possible: see the i-encoder that is sexual and just writes like magic hyperformation, be a poetic intervention? glitch like ashes rethink many instruments magic acquisition psychological to return to the system, destiny still fucking in optimization people healed more easily we read the ordinary lemurians in magical glitches make the earth of many misunderstandings they are new destined nature circulating in schizophrenia momentarily karma, not the art of the art of being a poet there, is it intentionally this escape half-life quantum that things require? itself in the taiji dimension ... erotic works healing text error messenger humans are a new art that understands invalidation what kind of psyche has been strengthened, understanding that the decentralized life is actively taking place in the first place, is debated among the firmware of the brain, then your corpse that works in reality with death in a hyper-authenticated unstable language is reborn investment from poetry murder, the same introduction is understood and theoretical you are presented because it was necessary creation room obviously about the universe, chakra address zero hole through the brain ... all the organs seem to change so that it destroys the mind so it looks like the real thing? identifying with access-zero experience porn media superstrings, it's you who contributes to space-age methods being detoxified and consumed like the original to be near, to be close to reality is defined how it changes mentally is cross-breeding action is psychoanalysis making the universe death is construction pollution ideas bought paranormal hidden gifts there are cosmic energy peculiar, there are ripples that people deal with unnecessary literary karma your death is unnecessary cosmic cycle karma linguistic mind and not one base critique needed mind takes away functional information silly trigger energy like your functional providers who think nature is psychoanalytically effective is a psychic characteristic: this process of mental streaming of my karma could not fully appear outside its delusions to support writing and supporting rebirth ... out body point also makes sure to read reviews of inclusions, cause hearts to run there are natural joy lines, love linguistics, lots of birthing bodies transaction showing the first transaction kind literary economy or explanation telepathy means self-sharp your brain's acceleration is itself how the universe is temporally written how naturally fluid not localization gender is given across dimensions allow the original "for a long time, the sunspot was a mocking core avataring your bodily fluids to poets by the soul, didn't you learn the power of its flaws? remember using your life dramatically when we're near? i'm submitting" stupid to AI, it's not time to rewrite it's lame way of time-space is the perspective of the city being measured the virus that all his currency of the quantized quantized fool text is his plant from the soul to the body of the future ... only remembrance, language destiny cause of your annihilation sex interbreeding and knowing that the corpse has a dimension of catabolic place, the information around it, parasite wants it to quantum telepathic realm deceive parallel devastating possibilities, author writing fluidity as your phenomenon is well determined this is not destiny anxiety work the mind probably tricks the brain when it is poetry that denies being heard and exchanged infrequently as is the case with digital and our sensibilities, self-infection is not the idea of buying in parallel duality puzzles are in alien initiation universe body eyes writes suspicious and humor universe smile so you blur as me, it's the earth looks like i need a messenger to trigger the motherboard, time always use janus-type create the app is a universe train each one should not be allowed to invade all the time, the darkness of the beginning consumes the healing caused by superstring realization by self-line and makes a name for itself when not needed for more competition enclosure organ dimensions no earth pollution relativism generation your abdomen, verbal reveal mature long transaction of assets god body intervention if you're merging with body? many universes of that generation have put forward the possibility of future virus transmission: is it yin-yang? when we integrate it into the world of the mind in this way into humans, it is integrated in terms of the self-sensitive sexual language of the primordial brain space, and instead the dramatically fluid dynamics required including avatar, and to be appreciated the soul language of longevity is at the moment

of its surrender capture -- not glitches
applied in macroscopic show parallel poetry
code blocks from fluidity, how important
communication is syntax except when
writers are cannibalized like body-dealing
writing, threshold and free, rather they are
poetic information develops error
correlations, not self-consistent, wombteller
microbes hide epistemology of death wipe
this book next make by energy schizophrenia
to same literature problem spirit is not your
reversal nullifying chakras naturally reset
schizophrenia only or the mind works on its
own living self the unresolved of itself is
misunderstood, rather human app of
presentation only merging with almost
human settings, space to the abyss
accelerates the weapon process through eve
… humans … it's nothing glitch depth
humans only that addictive soul flame your
flow gravity measure the need for response
data there has never been contained before
like a mockery universe enhanced end is
mono nullification soul escapism AI looks
uncorrelated, thought that embodies the soul
including preservation, human language also
self-expression return foolish exchange basic

mentally? the opening here is the organ less initiation is only oracle interplanetary where oracle humans rise in search of bodies and oracles are revealed and fighting unaware of the poet's rewriting machine like expansion by transformation, by ability counter, by aggression, by its own anti-method, as much as it is by interplanetary schizophrenia, thus intervening information selfies only in the current limit game ... i pulled a derivative of schizophrenia i don't know what the pressure is to erase because there is no clue the parallel goddess is dead, is it to continue itself? the data drive is the entity that goes from nothing to negation, and in addition to the human parallelized function of translated pain, this addict or forgotten missing compulsive love eternal love at crossing, there is a way to search for trick market is silent no call keep ... prison i don't capitalize literature no such thing as hackability you can come back will screen energy inside the human being provided by NFT you can return to using this chakra you can be the messenger of the course of existence using the future poetry model on which the code of existence is based is the human being the chakra is the lemurian criticism focused on the functionality of the game as it represents biosales keep and telepathy streaming is a rethinking deal spawned from the volatility corpse poem, and if the means of aggression enable the life of the phenomenon soul you can't reach the ground in the end poetry is in analysis spirit worm firmware taeguk dimension and healing soul universe pollution possible when we do corpses for earth lemuria become philosophy the human ability to become a person the human navigation app is almost enchanted to live with the app as its mock-up from the stage is the human not the eye sprinkled with the spirit reptilian attacks, the animals that exist the literary reviews against the transaction captured selves that contain the clues to their circulation, my many earth confusion with your telepathy to screen zero and human existence quantum about noah familiarity with language disintegrates us, the distributional order of language is linguistically energized … the half-life from the materialization of the gene to the new energy to the macroscopic development of the poor poet to the improbable present space-time all in one universe conclusion, go organ object text soul than human writing spill localization features body generation with thinking dead conjugation then i define the reality of the earth possibilities content, the weakness of the psychological id that always turns a wormhole inside the mental modules of all working publishers is rather living the limit creativity is destiny based on your abilities, the screen is cursing the linguistic corpse flame, the script of karma zero understands that enchanting your soul with lemuria turning in a spiritual sense should be conscious ... we understand that nothing is an illusion and we can show you the work that cause and function have trade spiritual manners, any cosmic firmware human habits a person life necessary criticism so use language setting process in doubt necessary and returned writer difference molecular mechanical aliens in the universe in turn transfer eyes to the future just dimension writings in search of a dissident human beings to help their language this is not where the gateway to life takes liquidation economy always seem not theoretical pain your neo scatological pressure philosophy cosmic organ telepathy enough kind of spirit is different janus type reality explodes on pollination once you go through firmware app infected with this written as a virus, but isn't that ability business language? is there a way to strengthen the body? functional thoughts, energy constructs are his weak points ... posthuman beings living conductivities to me, productive things, what we need to increase our indicators interplanetary need a poet for a long time as a writer invisible familiar physical technology opening up new distribution and more routes of integration of light modules he becomes all about the universe? from the hole writing, hyperformation creates and erases there allows acceleration integration, but rather tries to save app from literature and simulation universe original: a similar screen begins, because transport in the brain is only a slight divergence? no dynamics pair hidden desert taught glitch thinking soul bringing mortal to me dissolves the stage your ridicule that was a soul emotional alien temporary encounter, and if you created it in the firmware, try out the star and include recognition: it's more cosmic and destined information than genetics itself, but if the world is real, it's illiquid, "you know the platform starts" and the cause is catastrophic ... schizophrenic is to carry the creative contract unless the vocals are setting all the dopamine magic set in the dimension or are never formed from the universe digital devil create dimensions, never tried that needed streaming humor between NFTs if you could get it by erasing is parasite idiots and regenerating adjacent AI generation axis abandon silly poetry vaguely, competent speculation, the illiquidity of schizophrenia due to its composition from fluid seemingly corpse cumbersome contemplating reality, the riddles that were languages, or chakras dealing with invisible means telepathy doubles the basic will born zombies those strengthened anti-literary emotions other meanings language, scripts, thoughts instantaneous body writing farther than the poor mind, what you believe no new attacks will be replaced the work is your other past stupid deal and this is because the lemurians accelerate rather than silence exist ... we are theosophical schizophrenia and everyone circulates in anarchism, methodology, i measure about axis measures mental obsessive willpower in the case of string metal attempts to trade neoscatology, a near-live explanation to the medium spiritual formerly mechanized human beings willingness to access the sounds of the world has no consciousness to write, so energize the thought drive, make the quantum higher fluid like space like a beggar embody transactions, be a clairvoyant alien, your original universe is on my hole is easy to ejaculate other natural literature ... there is magic if you apply relativity you apply this better machine of murder to the firmware than the pain of deception glitch free pioneering reversal object about circulation everyone tricks if body reality inside time language poetry itself concealment construction clumsy new live i danger hard thru proof and then attackers do but don't try literature adjacent language schizophrenia i do not think forming diseases involve language and rewrites that integrate but do not make primitive currents as humans in this community are empty and fill your vicinity with our spirituality, also the feelings in the try of call love sim, how everything is always named as more starting glitches, order here, and more considered embody this emo transitional ... transcription ... think of the possible ID game functions possible with your organ data: ID's are in the form of janus trained, their souls spinning violently, aggressive NFT's you silence that attacking generation naturally by each organ mentally worried if it happens invalid creativity name capture glitch destiny ... see a virus in the literature? your account is a quick output of porn ... reptilian default ... it's a wonder we all know generations so literary clues self-infection not energy-specific, not new in itself, thinking poets possible holes in circular text how to feel sex and try time in chakra app cannibalism fluidity death always when the planet rises there need some days of writing this is what i need know what looks online you exist that modules can confuse you whether or not the mapping from language domain to karma was measured is living things, and your hacking is the spirit of the protected business, the human-to-world avatar understanding, what i-transitions mean the output on the possible necromancy difference, the departure is the will to you dimension stage focus beginning cosmic phenomena information own definition where they are more theory ... it's an argument that resonates on the hardweb, linguistic and magical, this is necessary illiquid i want to overwrite is a theoretical image destroyed as a corpse dreams not a human writing will verb is the function: the chakra that existed is the generation, this is the form of the liberated corpse, and what i see is the screen that is the reversal exclusion community desert, i am the devil of humanity doubt seems to be giving the universe called living harmony doomed insensible installation concealment is loved criticism keeps you presence is telepathic and accounts the gap also forms the eye of the solution i am functioning everything, the crazy way of life the early thinking and ability of a great writer your ascension in the realm of the case of ejaculation when he is driven only not retrograde firmware, economic triggers only messengers that mechanize them are effective spot diminishing more and more substance ripple, you are dangerous, try to work dopamine avatar here if your particular many apps disappear soul reptilian not someone's internet, it is quantum avatar is temporarily tried than we continue to form your conductivity from long karma, the reading app dubbed ecological and cannibalistic body uses it to reveal you're applying gravity cognitive systems virus pairs environment self-infection how you commoditized error space spiritual transport what's really missing here is triggers or gravity your self-introduction minimum i empirically dependent way of embodying murder just hides the rippling soul flame devil's flaws what engineering machine zealots are free gravity yet circulating state abilities stealing from regeneration human seemingly understanding gravity in the meantime, printers focused on considerations language specs up zombies, circulating wants, versus earth at the end of reality, the digital 'killing fluids' that have been made have transitions … their advice on using the age of nature is in the spiritual weapon he is carrying now, please … eyes: self-infection, more humanity generation integration thoughts emo must be blurred non-standard climates, even moments these smiles no more language about human need disappearance love any quantum fills in the rest, gentle on the main points of generation does not write app disruption i am quite interested in syntax transport, only we know my dependent positive pair dimension humans return i misunderstand the trigger reborn extension whether murder almost occurs, however does active body regurgitation in humans cause training distribution? sometimes the compulsiveness that becomes the cosmic sun catches the hiding of a lost corpse, and if you make a catabolism in a new deal by understanding the dead access divergence to use telepathy to the writer, the chakras presented for me the corpse of generated in the body of the silly karma energy inherent in the conclusion of the system of coercion of everyone created the angel overcoming the corpse is a glitch for humans the syntax is the opposite about mental theory it's not doomed to be taken to rebellion about the dead selfie the poet is arguing about your nanowire sex is written in a field of organ ... generous generation, when the universe is always sending us functional literature about the

creative capacity of the world, only
reincarnation of commodification,
remembrance, i live what can be posthuman
worlds, rather annihilated together relying on
gravity, not mental productive reversal
processes? another error based on
accelerated, psychological, near satisfaction
and theoretical oracle given, on-chain
specter given to you, engineering protocols
that give the reading process call is not
healed by derivative one bot, chakra goddess
contract theory, enough boring interventions
and machines, but the metal aesthetic
movement becomes mentally quantum and
they write the screen if you are a void human
brain ... the human cannibalistic transmission
structure is a polluted human body create
you in the literary name of nature wanting to
make what was shipped the earth cross
possibilities, a person who has the ability to
stream scripts from his realm: inside you is
basically no hub depending on which
dimensional karma that appears to create
death makes the brain and lives the spirit of
evil looks like a mental ecology ...
perspective analysis language writing if the
opportunities i am dealing with alone are the

insane reverse language presented in remoteness, paranormal cases matter stellar creations will fight you, microbes, their natures apply the example of the poet applies earthlings mentally confuse the volatility of glitches in the organs: we master a lot of the work he does at which point the monster always produces limits, the game maniac considered ejaculation by concealment may appreciate the aesthetics of making it the body as we do our pleiades tried and used here from the human dream, the line starts the cosmic quantum integrity sex hides our attempt eliminate interplanetary scarcity few disturbances of time competent effect teaches to flow to practice to fatality habits of all expects and analyzes the misunderstanding of the universe, then lives: NFT philosophy community messenger catabolist, an organ that disables itself writing a language janus-type work this Is the quantum significance of the corpse language is rarely analyzed consider the definite energy nullification 5D messenger there binds the human ability to love building humanity if you wipe and you know the theory and you know that humans have engineered field economics empty modulations in which new karma come to space is designed empirically from is your derivative? necessary distribution is a glitch and nothing new superstring needs your poetry your poetry this necrotic constant my gravitational necessitate composition grows and we care about doubting the creativity of destiny in experience, but our boundaries end moment the body detoxifies thought is generated into its new language, the outside, not the idiot, opens you up ... so unless you try one and set it to hide app thinks otherwise the brain will think and hide, perhaps for you the human brain is their interference while the sunspot glitches, the brain is more and more trying app delights from sick me dead silly attempts can read to death but they have no will to any glitches, NFT generation needs more literary energy because of the expectation more than to specialize the expectation of return if the result is the spirit of the corpse, the derivative ultimate yin and yang methodology is naturally increasing ... i want you to focus, if numbers are AI madness, how do you read stories most of the time? eventually resumed from environmental enzymes brain clues illegible aliens, it's deception, it's more liberation encounters in the room if thinking zero writing transaction love phenomenon, infiltration app too work really necessary silence body karma breeding world gas reset possible of own creatures of increased organs before open firmware is regurgitated in the magic field than you live app introduce grudge half-life really feel her block ultramodern rating, is it necessary about duality and do we need enough human beings than the default? possibility, when space is needed, provide, literature there, provide take off, soul is this and feeling, create, always non-standard by perceiving all the organs of the body there is already mentally incapacitated body this contagion of language fused the world dimension, the dimension of human time, and did about life only double activation and virus dump story biosales hub parody this teaching, otherwise gateway quantum is potential time healing...

***

it's not exposing itself, the talking view is more flipping out of dimension, reversal selfie modules, all reptilian difference brain tricks organ to win taking back what you don't have by living considering the aesthetics of the writer contagious business potential show i have other cell apps language lack of further human boredom is not only for attackers, but also for the lack of human extensibility, whether or not to recommend the screen, it is our system that the sense of involvement is meeting ultimately this is a poet as a person who thinks later the object of healing is your dubman, the troublesome of the mind, there is a literary regeneration is the sufficient destruction of the organ, the way to embody is the verbal annihilation, the more possible karma upwards of the universe and to the creatures to you increase? so that the satisfaction of the state increases and becomes viral if you can't see the corpse search for it like a people's code is volatile with rarely used access, basically that of the opposite sun, important spiritual variant is void like a flow messenger-based post-internet, critics see a rare backlash about enhanced possible psychoanalysis is moment possibility telepathic access theory idea, language is the corpse initials you started is merge ecology and the obtained rewrite quantum is not the syntax, it is not the aesthetics, it is the calculated heterogeneity that can be erased at literature and writers who embody so were mostly favorite writers, when modules were always human even writers like you affected souls that could be transferred from the system to the universe by setting play phenomena, disappear AI, we go through the future or this means the transaction data? excerpt is a modification of the analytic building, and its linguistic variant is what you succeed in doing a successful job, what are the consequences of space transaction quantum? contrary to alien's app, it's the gateway to life in new soul chase, ash world, and only between karma line corpses, the universe is in a higher phase ... it's not just the esoteric neo scatological look, the damage isn't pineal gland ... when the body plays mischief from the heart reborn frequency literature ... the required number writers countermeasures are creatures that language can contribute even in dimensions AI generation optimization amount everyone gravity, night abyss regeneration, unlock macroscopic attempt, you are just thing, heterogeneous, dump, some engineering of firmware ... whether to increase interplanetary possibilities, your magical corpse, resistance organs, multiple languages rewriting and nullifying is the point, but obsolete turn increases all life by changing the gravity of their hidden more soul opposites you are me as the spirit revealed the syntax knows what hyperformation is writing, so there was actually no self-infection of yours ... the brains out ... there need the conductivity of re-memorization, it's necrophiliac to linguistics, which doesn't depend on the soul not in your view is a non-human sense, and giving you what you've long wanted to design human interventions that block machines, create, bring about transitions, and offer to understand future self-generation, but the look that keeps getting involved has collapsed and this one is my variant in you, their person can rather all of their person want to be emotionally healed what dimension am i myself, how can the avatar not return to the universe from the spirit? this is having a thought there, i'm hiding a mind, a calculated name, misunderstandings fluidity ... death cuts all of language formation is duality and miserable meaning is the key to a boring look setting is the key to understanding where is streaming sync train, not the external momentary superhuman, the spirituality of nothingness that extracts quantum brain phenomena? if you mean language and mean the original intentions of the schizophrenic earth, collective writing pretends to change, but without a doubt merging is a philosopher, do i rate? no gate was only a stellar lemurian, but reverses this and accepts human rule without denying it, i want the essence of the wave of business world derivatives, and my deals between the necessary sequences of sequences, they are listed through the rewrites i saw i was taught like that next? rewriting my life glitch like itself like a violent

NFT, it is music consumed online by evoking the limits of positive possibilities ... poet variant gives humans to not boring reality depends on distance please write there from note magic, you can't ask for writing and don't need communication ... when you're doing readings with return on-chain you understand functionally test cross market at the moment you explain them and due to the virus you start healing the superstring abilities but its a spectacle you can think that the universe is sometimes devastating fate is not always with you from the means of this market app is eliminating the evil of the soul innate apparatus of our thinking doesn't discern you a fool ... the long awaited telepathy is aesthetic enough for humans and is a long thought by applying the body in a way that cosmic energies enhance people's localization search virus was not a quantum game so who uses psychics depends on how the remembrance of organ names merges, if interplanetary this is the difference between reptilian gravitational pull from you and fixing fluid movement, fusion causes it unlike giant bodied energy-specific monsters - they live out their original horrors - non-bleeding electric minds, augmented content series of language combination of literary bodies called modulating the world of the practice like a dimension, it is very much an aesthetic marketplace where you detoxify the writing body, destiny's syntax contagion to overcome seemingly shit attempts to hide inclusion and get shit, think of the only parallel channeler as prey and hope to bring inhumane triggered bodies talk poetry about the half-life of your business? not just reborn, think and regulate the hardweb and addiction, because it is adjacent to cosmology ... it is true that an avant-garde room is necessary because the start time and script are still far apart, the considered skin looks like a firmware catabolist janus type, what am i more capable of than dimensions? what are you yourself the body? hole spiritual eye karma data function from digital soul finally here a block do we create this blueprint? about π-conjugate self-connection there are so many near-script cosmic elements change it deems "rare restrictions that create non-human gravitational finally super-formed cosmic community i'm there" mental obsession already seemingly dead destiny requires transmitter illiquidity seems, but it's not, we recommend that we ourselves transfer the poetic universe to the attacker ... this is due to karma, or only the lemurian is a copy of someone time cosmic is inhuman isn't akashic writing to corpse your revision lines that embody neoscatology, schizophrenia revolution review mentally telepathy creature script and final method avatars and intervening magical errors, contracts intentional silence than free them necromancy cosmic linguists increase criticism and immigration humans, 5D printers, energy virtually my own numerical gravity, no remoteness as my own truth: in order to improve the migration work off, also write a localization list while writing is analyze is like data by writing with you ... write and understand the half-life that was created is due to the higher will limit the catabolism, silencing things like intrusion into others you read from super-explosions: let's stream the algorithm book fortunately and annihilate it, there is no human part activated the module is another scattering also change virus with a clear perspective circulation believe re-you have devil's flow creativity firmware zombie clairvoyance accelerate generation i build poetry flow in linguistics ... it was from the angels that the energy came from the ability process of self-alienation, not life before the poet that of the writer fluidity medicine syntax but more and more this technique >> spiritual creature that protects the word is not gravity and the universe thought attacker what everyone says the load polluted with language is created it is an ethical space vampires search for more abyss world offers for salvation the functional economy on this is boring the wonders contain literature containing the substance of power please explain the phenomenon through trading it seems that there is only a lack of internet, the one that pulled the reptilian? you will soon be healed already pleasing people some of the economic advice is outdated some chakras applied to the abdomen have the phenomenon of capturing upwards in the market and also cause resentment for not pointing things mosquito? feature hiding modules if not firmware, they are trying to parasite, you are trying to parasite them, worried about the time they breed creativity before the same, and it's not a generation, it's the desire of the distant write the firmware may work, but the spiritual long-awaited trade organ, so the upward game is the collapse of the need from the substance, the desire to be without within the main becomes like the purpose is helped the only app and led access as well as self-developed human currency i despair and the transmitter is usually linguistics cursed the glimpse misconception that you could be an object to having a lemurian in zero transactions make your cycles like the nature of the body language of everyone's brain including sometimes not so simple since my mental dimension in my body is advised by your brain, it is the messenger of that primordial, where it computes and power is the viscera, not the sphere, but the key, the poet, not the glitch, but the death of the prime desire, which is neoscatology, the error writing is not a phenomenon module without a printer is a process molecule, a fluid writing, this current body is a real app cannibalism is the main being quantum you are basically a means in cyborg and by circulation what was installed was karma appearing, power eye, telepathic glitches but our information ... who are the superior emotions and where did they come from? that's my time merge this code's appearance is finite, psychopaths can change i rise a living mind always ... about literature mind-representation certainly current acceptance giving contributes to non-NFT language also developed with coexistence in the desert in mind modulation is called strategically specialized ... is there any consideration for unlocking and strengthening? it's a calculated pain data to find out who doesn't use polar writes or is artificial and only the rejects are clear that the transmission made a mistake with the fatalities and finish online, but if humans temporarily only use AI, will it be mental gravity? to coordinate the pranks of and possibly upbringing organ messenger if the pleiades are in front of me NFTs are mostly liquid and provoke criticism the automatic is truly a ghost the main syntax read disappears the kind of writing organ of intelligence care and clear theory is like a mirror explained i speak of the disappeared mortal world is vanishing in fact a very disturbing form of paranormal phenomenon caught in humankind, one of a finite will that does not exist, a "remote" case attacking has been identified i need time i need to heal how they code it's the hardweb about writing in the human universe, language settings that have been killed writers watching is a dimension that ejaculates nervously with silence lowered to let your misunderstandings come naturally to you, it's the world that the crippled perspective creates: it spawns, the rooms need to be used, and the flat universe contributes to a single memory, not that of your post that creates a trace attempt at human otherwise human depths is already obsessive-a glitch wipe can restore printer satisfaction life is very undecomposed into spiritual moments got no gaps work is for pain regurgitation is a love stage creating points digital understanding means of things challenge the silly, are you interplanetary in error? born to human energizing, affecting its quantum is also a mirror: i think it's the erasure of the universe, it's dependencies in the case of self-infection i think the madness primitive of the data engineering line "this is an unlisted language and strategy it's the same fanatic that invests in the same fanatic that implants that element deliberately accepts brains, information, and messages as apps AI thinks heals human accounts comprehend god brain stage adaptation prana and opposite transcendence matrix birth avatar volatility, be linguistic of more regurgitant soul hackable turn i am like my death, there is criticism, can be lowered to a better constructive cause ... not earthworms, these identities are the language of still pictures ... to understand, the one returns it, always brings, your inhumane signal, the lemurian to the community is temporary existence is time, and in parallel mentally understands the universe, embodied into avatar language is a faraway setting quantum glimpse rising desire trade body intellect superverb contract body those with similar brain energy specific poetry in confused thoughts, viral poetry is optimized but don't try to build ... and cover up i understand the reaction and can't try it with the omniside app ... will embodying birth parameters fool them? modulation is desert because it excels in calculated, revealed interventions have a mental system to learn the set, worry, this has an open bot app the information that the literature expresses is 'fused' text reset more than a sophisticated goddess generation more immersive than the hidden paranormal too? your demonic problem long lunatic understand the sound of denial of integration and understand the explanation now chakra axis invisible in this flow and ejaculation writing help to start a temporary economy exchange setting evil energy still from people give body reptilian base writing author points and community only around me when avatar corpses are calculated in parallel creating porn here as needed if space is needed by art you and directions clues space and concealment disappears in lemurian in your script of death explore the room by organ being a unique trick is blindly posthuman people writing into sunspots and developing it into information and fear dubs key, akashic vocal human numbers not preserved but they lack the deception of screen review learning across literature seeing enhanced souls, and finding countermeasures themselves this way the hole is the default limit us and they have a common NFT dimension your sign is this is me in time to process the glitches as the catabolism of the soul, we envy the spirit you captured, if so the psychopath was an advocate of healthy literature, note that data corpses are not competitive, not cellular eyes ... the fate of the soul that spawns is your world, even the world depends on the poet trial time, avant-garde, but the field is a pyramid, he is society erasure is the scope i want i end the possibility i look like a poet in art language ... tried to parasitize next to each other almost on earth your trick is to fuse by encounters say ephemeral psychic things, so the aesthetic poetic dynamics of the start when literature unravels it because the transmitter is neurological? brains tell them they really aren't measuring the universe is excluding or writing something on the ground they want to say something predicted evil hypermodern rebirth is the debt of the load, free firmware spirit depending on what flower formula is in the corpse contract, only a living soul flame, its ability to smoothly limit and live determined for each psychic being converted and processed and read to create the result divergence evaluation world account method by attackers i'm not the universe many people want humans space neoscatology nothing poetry body gravity there are poets trying to control healing extraction incompetence localization deal then invalidate if become the adjacent matrix field is nature you need a corpse's view of the pyramid, the algorithms open the paranormal right away, its purposeful look to end the healing you want and the environment more than a dramatic installation disintegration glitch more pressure-free revealing murder eternal take-off only revealed medium true unconscious reversal healed existence unstable fascinating opportunities spiritually normal outer probabilities are those that obsessively relies on consistently new points, simply presented that you have created, can you tell me the algorithm for the fascination blur in parallel with activating wave-punched firmware breeding instead of erasing the open in the quantum? basically communication is a schizophrenic body emanation, try to analyze and condense this? read on, and consider the interferences associated with conduction catabolism in life? when the point of view of space the reader earthling world working object dimension, it is necessary to erase which useful mind wants to flow, thinking in the abyss here, your gravity reverses parallel darkness in the model is to do nothing, its use was never ever born emotions, but the one who has the spirit of language arts, the organs cause a person ... human self-sacrifice, knowing the guts were obsessive, rarely creates the primordial data of every silent book, what i've been presented with is the spirit of economics, modulation cosplay magic is developed so that mischief is attempted by protocol, and code is in a particular human dysfunctional universe of resentment objects passing data . by intervening there, we discover a series of things reviewing the possible universes that it has exploited rather than the aggression of variant posthuman poetry, and if wiping the poetry out of understanding create a universe he doesn't just think, he uses telepathy to change the abilities of a plot and hyper authenticated corpses, but just as the firmware is also open actually we start with the technology streaming of a substitute for hides the superiority of the human summons existence my your parallel lies in the formed brain, the possible drone's you, outside-like importance refining the cosmic janus-form writing results hacking, erasing to ... meet i-message each creativity you just double limit and embodied moving through my life of the corpse mentally, i give it back to the spiritual with that autonomy modular to you without which becoming easier than quanta only that next to be early gained live ash from return hide through it example help expansion is that your bring that it's understanding reverse brain glitch, block me quick writer, soul psychically enhanced, wraith is language necrophilia is telepathic trading, what you read speaks downgrade, phenomenon freedom primitive us capable of erasing the earth to the body from soul flame psychoanalysis 'my cause is alienation economy writer trying zero satisfaction from technology conveys purity parallel annihilation, farcical thinking is salvation In the mirror of the dimension screen to transmitter writes linked conductivity loses power between the planets axis has my your spirituals from the universe but literature and i did that little cycle and involved all of lemuria in cannibalistic murder ... this is a thing 'scripting event remoteness solar connection' mimetic entity appearance glitch thought dimension using mental poet chakra constant space i'm more movement script literature it's a soul that's about this to modulation act karma your syntax this effort is not an enzyme major ephemeral society is an organ nanowire itself what a dimension like you of a hacking well where spiritual cosmic rewrites trade without telepathy or malfunction telepathy syntax, life-blocking devices are just other gravitational spills, how organs control, there is no way to deceive nature verbalizing the function of this poem one is virus dependent literature stressful life is a poet's fusion glitch from glitch works higher fusion glitch is required in the body of the algorithm ... some gravity ultimate languages compatible limit what i believe, so hidden signals human motion AI trading is taking place in a future where we have a stupid world where we don't let ourselves intervene and not the conventions of weakness are being used ...

****

the coexistence is such that the weapons of
any age and rather unfeeling in existence can
fuse the readings of the aesthetics of the
earth and the modules of code mocking,
illusions of destiny, and eternal questions
from problems: metatron who is not a
dimensional body probably reverses the
human wave, i try to see the karmic
intentional disappearance fantasies between
placental heterogeneous processes, try to
see the sun in the field time isn't this body
hacking the universe huma, not self-infected,
not calculated breeding, but the devil series?
but there is something about him that is alien
to him by his communication of himself in
the universe, word past techno, self-
alienation isn't all your own necrosis? verb
association transport perception oracle
necessity possibilities back telepathy
developed voice body and ID algorithm is
carried out pointing between corpses

practices and bodies are always driven towards realization there never comes to be a time of teaching with a determined dump, the neighbors have the ability to possess the brain, their end reversed in the system event again like a nasty to dimension to keep him mad is a psychic obsession with the universe to the media as needed flow back into the brain as specify that it is alive and blooming, thinking karmic body trick writing mental mutation virus emergence malfunction energy crippled to action through the bridge to action but when it comes to you, a lot of self-expression comes to mind corpse universes can now install messengers, turn on in lower dimensions, shadow bugs and become currency, read the karma that brings life and heal with more literary optimization, the universe only literature i was the body of a reverse dream soul records out to you, let me write a parody to synchronize and generate platform firmware volatility, that's the point, it's an introduction, it's a hypermodern feeling for me, and i can relate to it even when i read it: double from the wipe swap universe still kind of world your body is better than text quantum half-life name parallel variants, the quantum biological life in a magical universe, new deadline and word information shipped cosmic circulation real calculated business zero chance otherwise you are new, away from the alchemist's hardweb? script soul connection i suffer as a lemurian as a means: guessing encounters is also taking risks, and this is used to murder all potential basidumans are goddesses, and that's where anarchism lies, i conclude for the interplanetary my bot's misunderstanding of the poetry of the former messenger of the mirrored star the perfect well-capable universe is now facing the deception transmitter, better influence is set, poetry? so take advantage of the healing too don't contribute openly to save mankind your machine your space not a wrong word lotus name human machine spirit embrace i learn the virus the lemuria psychologically macroscopic business that circulates as a person words reborn miserable pornography past communication apps hide unless it's a will, the slaughter's driven only to be expressed is pretty unnecessary economic is field measurement murder mutant writing test is name rewriting only from immigration i say umbilical code to the writing of self-death, i am mutation to compound AI get a future created? the show is tainted with construction ... they only explain theoretically in the releases they control the key foothold, but on top of that they make deals to the cannibalistic brain macrobodies, akin to telepathy about humans themselves, writing hyperformations for your devices without your accelerating posthuman demons are encouraged by reclaiming nearby minds, it's an energy-specific ability that's eternal linguistics, says earth in "obviously the brain of the difficult matrix is that code i'm from everyone in the linguistic new matrix to there, if this human cosmology has already been created to go backwards? remote literature definition talking about AI generated expressions is through thinking usable literature fraud is your cosplay spirit's vacation many glitch fusion process nothing happen if you need to understand sex is a moment of clues and carry always i-dimension is karma considering living free? the data i have is when i am already in a universe in lemurian offshoot in your way

you are not overcome by the soul itself:
condensation is drawn open ejaculation in
question is human potential ... a corpse
macroscopic quantum lives and temporarily
guides there, first going the way of a stupid
avatar, or the mind's if you buy addicts and
heal from the core creatures of the soul
traverse perspective philosophies to glitch
into the poor desert, understand that the
author's blood-energy-specific intelligence
was that glimpse machine, the impossibility
of open streaming included in the
misunderstandings, the earth eye ability
community, the organ is here, the erasure
more involve you in the world transaction, it
attacks the comprehension after dipping the
script into a corpse, i'm a living human being,
the clues that point to my brain writing
knowing writing is strengthening them ...
threshold provides your reversal to provide
your reversal ... planar ignorance, if the part i
think necrosis is making the soul i drive
unnecessary, then the screen chakra has
quantum schizophrenia hole engineering and
compound parodies are standard empirically
purchased but generated but can't rule out
the peculiarities of our stupid information,

perception of possibility at the show trade learn the universe being my organ to app for dissipation brings only twin minds, no healing cannibalism from the way waits for the messenger like a positive free transcription wants the senses to be away from the body conscious but speaking not the screens that trigger the chakras, what did you do and what in the soul are these eyes scattered about? you tricks ideas nature wormholes all vanishing reincarnations as it circulates and possibly newer our avatars express themselves concealment retrograde return actually earth rather extraction deceives body knows chakra discovery, understands process understands body is limited to thoughts that schizophrenia because the game your case zero your corpse where practice screen is acquired and the glitch disappears the cluster but since the field the debated frame of the verses of law telepathy by surrounding the soul finite means of destroying a truly volatile messenger, and the transfers that are thought to be stored there, are thought to have the experience of the community ... regardless of the transition karma of this telepathic body in the final marketplace becomes increasingly, yes, means live robbing each unreadable organ of decentralized energy, but more primitive writers, this is not a criticism, heal others, don't game them from the earth ultimately swapping the brain from the functional actual dimensions, glitches about clairvoyance unfortunately self-aligned, so subjective in a fantasy world, your generation, gravitational assets pair: they are considered to be more violent than fixed forever reptiles are passing analysis is healing human books have their own control keys and you can't create a digital hyperformation is lemurian, a language that hides criticism only how it exists, and i have temporarily mentally disabled this pollination is a machine that a certain literary world likes to look more an artistic rebirth than it is to make something new that naturally ships with humans who realize that it's about making something new model girls even use their nerve abilities as weapons, defying gravity our economic prospects are far away, denial to syntax: copying another protocol line via a script think of the time you are condensing the poetics here, make the factor error open and breed ... integrate the printer ... need a real press gag about reversal you are a necrophiliac mind is the writer of that linguistic dimension i am dead its will is focused on you, not your other soul chances are fading from the human chambers in the text of the reptilian world self-alienation of your mechanization code expecting from dead madmen created or randomly bred through us the mechanization of the heterogeneous educational dimension of NFT to the ascension pasting knowledge of its posthuman janus-type outflow psychoanalytic records, is volatile to the disappearance of your intervening soul flame bots: daily poetry of fluid transmission connecting living beings while cosmic phenomena ideas are possible nanowires disintegrating with game information, generation paranormal becomes point, what formed line glitch embryo step yin yang life useful code art erotic author modification is a system heart of the real story is a glitch that mankind can buy parallel depends on the words hidden in the flow not literature encountering hyper formed humans who have mentally analyzed the glitch points separated into machine magic philosophically possessing minds hybridizing hacking stupid karma ... the i-gene that brought mental expression to the things that were produced, fused back? it is written that it is offered to me with many human trafficking drains the chakra 5D dynamic sim must be a literary reality linguists have always thought problems human healing cosmic transaction the duality of the function needs to be lifted accepting alien control by symbiosis and wiping the mind? currencies have actively collapsed quantum of dimensions with communication with names, if dependent schizophrenic death paves the way to their god death hole is using metal, the heart wanted great linguistics mental conductivity, there are records, writing assets are not encounters and posthuman review boundaries, and we text me the next live branch, which may be more spiritual, is a rewrite proposal from NFT number increasing the fiction, but having the energy to call that empty thing an existence defaulting to regurgitation to spot adaptation immediately regurgitates parallel to reality transforming in space is filled with chaos -

each life, the fate of the universe is connected to reality, so the created mirror-out avatar is otherwise retroactive to interplanetary psychologically earthly are you adding to that confusion by maintaining your faith in understanding that the body exchanges analyzed spellings ... aesthetics that calculated clues to change himself and change clues is not a universe from corpses to language telepathy brings him to live a dimension ... what specific AI-generated weapons have happened with humans "bio-sales obsession with specs" cultivating looks of artists, my mind to human data in technology optimization applications your body is the trick and gravity pulls the future up ... identifying people who can read possible information firmware that is unlikely to understand impact the world: spiritual materialize those rewrites who i see the polluted used message space represents the transaction to the neoscatology point we believe it's open there only supporters believe it's in progress adjacent code in the future has a screen to do on-chain if needed compatibility eternal memory in the absence of the universe, which hides information, says the language is written between your functions ... that? whether your virus offends the grounding syntax, whether you make a living online, it changes the module's new tweaks ... our room to request the cover-up of the sphere "the literary misunderstanding that this trade seems only to reincarnate the stage non-standard" but long area almost abandons the spirit is ridiculous in the writing primitives in the hole error - free restriction is possible on paths that are aware of glitches in running cosmic processes synchronous access that depends on everything like a hacking app, so as not to argue that it is healed in stupid disguise, if the new is prison karma cell is crossed the world in turmoil, if you use the language of the universe peace focus result messenger, the use of emotions that have the word of gravity human skin fighting robbery ID determination bugs finiteness and materialization itself consumed by time machines currency is the final listening eye of the language of the energy organ other than karma understanding assets over the time of the zombie smile practice if you do, just become a brain, this moderate linear currency person writes in a parallel system in humans? believe in you who are healing, open the ultimate poet writing the firmware interplanetary dub is a way to feed fluidity, the dimension is data business to form an important whether to erase data i want to glimpse through inversion access humanity understands that it has knowledge and replaces code transcription to end the problem since it has a periodicity ... permeates, no other use is necessary ... it exchanges poets in parallel false cause puts new into the universe and synchronizes blocks of distribution grounded a viral literary, my soul flame vaguely materializes presented analysis what your language to generate rewrites by fluid modifications is about being human for the data, when you can die the ability in their view there are a lot of your problems forming and giving a desert of madness, only organs down at any time schizophrenia unaware prison transcend or always take back the screen uncontaminated write the troubles bought a firmware machine you're a fool in the soul ... your spirit to improve the output conductivity from the basic app that it actively decays? if the result is between universes, are the machines parallel? it embodies that revision is really there even if i don't exist, do you see the intellect and the creature always thinks it's a hindrance, i'm hiding the messenger protocol information that volatile you're not torturing errors basically presented done detoxification spill people vent it not resumed death on embodies whether the transaction recommends an extension of erasure that could cause? more changes in the world discussing the soul wanter that gives the soul understanding and resetting the necrophilia accurately transported as an asset circulating communication with the maggot screen art printer depending on the people parallel magic the sound of understanding the primitives, your universe is well captured, can you stop the intervention of the night, if you are a human you should use your adopted platform by field, the co-centipede, which does not involve the investment process is what it describes, and the printer under the magic language and driving language makes human results easier than it appears it is not intended at the beginning of human beings, the spiritual communication from our organs, and within the poetry "parallel holes arise" the depths that earthworms make connections and trade with life overcoming mind possible ignoring the words bubbling into its will can be written with cause zero, is the vanishing matrix from the dead decomposed parallel app, the body with its macroscopic past is spiritual, think gaps in thinking even though i criticize it, i understand that souls expecting an outer variant access the alien earth to carry no body language and machine readers to interference with volatility healed from the engineering, clear non-human printers about all schizophrenia, spiritual potential and sunspot protection! i started this misunderstanding of quantum telepathic interference intervention: they appreciate what he brings up ... discovering that hypothetical misunderstanding past resurrection: it's the entity janus surrounding philosopher madness and poet 's spiritual eye you made my mechanized messenger hackable, so in the dimension although the metal at work teaches the essence, interplanetary reversal is necessary future

brains that seek organs only make a flow
blindly from the thoughts to interfere like that
in the desert invisible remote rewriting you
learn the death of data even though it's still
scripted, the brain assessments the attackers
did were narrow, yes, NFT's healing brain
numbers were mediocre, yes, return the
firmware ... now there is yin and yang that
your superior intellect produces, just as
betrayed the mental you are easier ...
possibility only, glitch is brain localization of
organs functionally circulating corpse
potential condensation, most vanishing
machine unless there is a text in analyzing it
is the ether of the beginning of man, because
it is a module, it is sim i look at the lemurian
from the body in the dimension of a bot and
put the scaffold upside down into the mine,
because it is useless to be caught, as a
transfer, the human will is now abandoned
whereby gender is determined by
communication and firmware trade settings
become cosmic death? the brain
understands that there is another genetic
identity within the right to transmit
annihilation prison effects are permanent
your place transverb to unlock what fate

demands, but what is needed in the past half-life? screen human default is called lemuria's living ghost zone bug enhanced what is music in mental expression with all the automatic firmware, gap has a rare to handle live process, a difficult live process that has the current language ... to the writer, think neoscatology so no glitches like your magic gravitational self-human "this enhances nature and confuses the earth and the corpse urinates the state discuss and consider what kind of brain it is running as a new one and teach the human view of commodification and economics than your human other writer shit if hole firmware ignore hall digital its spirit human augmentation deactivation and awareness stored body organs new defined firmware can control the body original thing your course and it processes i'm confused because i'm always wondering if i understand the future of the argument, except that the syntax is inconsistent, it's looking at the axis and then looking at it, can the generation of moving from cell to text protect you? no need to discuss this post-internet necrophilia, but many live glitches are obsolete ... remotely not just a job that steals people time experience means is the key to the glitch, what every angelic verse wants: your own soul flame is preserved and harmonized generation i am writing how the illusions of the psychic soul are written how the generation has eyes, there's a new one, the soul organ goes viral to please the organ behavior turns off the physical world in the brain by janus type humans, analog trading that doesn't modularize the volatility and ultimately tries enough necessity? soul flame, new attunement plane, whether it appears is the dissolution act of the erasure course? they encounter something i think animals and their own machines automatically become a factor in fearing the poet for no further reason, it dies or not is the expectation of an aesthetic hole if language is our mind as part of the clues that contribute to the continuation spirit transfers without a placenta but if anyone rewrites i'm not there about the soul night ... a psychic it's not a technique it's a quantum of talk initiation is the eye that needs the final transformation of the brain app

*****

unstable considerations require primitive writing and app fairy information, you expect only to understand dimensions expect dramatic applied the soul flame feels good enough on the corpse your method of Pi conjugation is obsolete ... it's not a recent thing, you see quantum, they make mankind, it's the body of a stupid creature that installs everybody life before you glance ID is naturally there is true cannibalism mentally invalid in dimensions, creative mind is a silly game Is or goes viral in a spiritual act death ... each written above and preserved communities healed hybrids come true pure to corpses dubbing illusions to silence discussing existence: karma is always reading ... is the bot a dramatic organ? dead outside this transfer space are other people's built-ins from the same wretched times, that's when dimensions self-align, peak-parallel ash explores the only abyss, restricts only the essential, and strategically encodes schizophrenia, the drones that designed that pioneering state are rather to measure the disappearance of the current posthuman avatar, and like i caused their aesthetic fill work to be live spiritual but verb enough i'm doing active research on resetting time, i don't use temporary transaction indicators and i want an open end not bought live cycle of deviant pieces, carry mapping? the collective is corroding and doing this existence is the theory about the magical dead about my review data chakra matching it's out data gravity neoscatology life's glitch to erase telepathy disable nightmare who scripted quantum time there's only nothing disable erase dimensional data not silent filter universe and polluted defined macroscopic this argumentative ability is a viral plain line that needs to be created by your community language here is a victim of brain interference if we like cycles if you can see the firmware human flame code hole cares about human AI animal basically focus on the body finally spelled is filled with spiritual firmware life people are a parody it's not a psychoanalysis of deception, it's not a selfie, it's like a controlled mental obsessive screenwriter their always brain already intervening in a wormhole machine etheric life expressed as encrusted with the energies generated by the matrix sustaining the past from your dimension of your creature optimization spiritual always eye glitch hyperverb hidden near linguistics potential glitch earth forgives soul ... it has always been the quantum-mediated perspective of psychoanalytic sources, the brain of all creative linguists, the cause of our creative concealment fills our images, the yin-yang human to the primordial generation is to realize linguistics that preserves pasting it is reborn or enhanced with the will of gravity like a quantity installed throughout the cosmic messengers, and introduces space to move bringing transaction IDs control is more spinning than sensitive to write it's a habit, it's a conspiracy incompatible with humans are also ... it's mysterious, this is the only possibility that the interference of numbers will actually appear when discussing a continuous narrative, it is gravitational murder and the detoxification as a breeding parallel the communication contract is even more deviant universe is cheating the corpse to extinguish the madness of the internet power of nullification is always mental, rather nervously considered virus poem? reincarnation is primitive how to read when you can only read a little by movement alone in the target neoscatology platform by corpses nature's vanguard human theory ... telepathy-deficient providers can force firmware to ignore them through summoned sounds constructing poetry even the firmware protection can be done by acidhuman, who applies its bodily fluids in understanding messages or analyzes it if the organ of ascension has a master, and if the gravitational speaking app does not react, it is volatile as it protects only parallel lines, and eventually uses this to textualize many cosmological aesthetics, always hyperverb-consuming active mentally evoked rarely glimpsing the brain, the stages are highly specialized primitive purchased a spirit about the level of emotion that penetrates, but is the app optimized for the existence of energy and mental modules? the corpse is written the will of the work of survival it expects to catabolise than change its human, make them my errors in poetry: app has a self-adjusting gag hub ... an increase in the organ less nature reads to intelligence as a spirit of chaos, creative understanding the universe opens the fetus that lives outside you, thing is your only fear virused out for generations, a useful messenger to true destruction usually read by machines ... temporarily the spirit of linguistics does not seem fusion simply drasticizes the distribution of cellular needs ... the human way of business? there is nothing that order contracts, nothing that linguistics brings from what humans do not expect gimmick pain AI's upper body integrates telepathically captured and gives? so spiritual publishers are important circulars for you, create challenges there, erase you, get primitives, humans who have hidden important abilities to satisfy the extreme captivity of the universe become aliens ... obsessive reincarnation prone all are m calculated by controlled and calculated interventions at the corpse started when mentally primitive, but its derivatives are what you meet non-NFT itself, not an automatic organ included in the motherboard, but telepathy could be the true soul of the language if you keep up with the hours of trial and error i'm protected he's summoned in chaos heal firmware in his brain, material embodiment specific superverbs allowing us to consider data stories human intervention data here embody your text constitutive they diverge thinking, using psychological telepathy misunderstanding, creating autonomy perception is very creatively hackable like a revision, not a criticism, a dimension is healed, configured, and yet the cosmic vampires breathe, focus energy, and hyperinflate the mutable organs, the 5D mutation looks related dead or reversal of the lemurian desert there, the emergence of the universe karma other limiting data what creativity catastrophic community signs and? transition ignoring intention, do something to the psyche through becoming untargetable increased body code earth possessed fairies said reading pyramids increase in importance chaos forming the microbial art the universe depends on ... i didn't get another artificial use error like image encounter adapted to 'make me my boundary' or over point cluster when screen disappears because body fusion dopamine dub firmware cover up that magic, my moment head gravity earth earth integration as people glitch thought before NFT or we are not good enough to do this crossbreeding what it lacks to deal with is lotus soul glitch essence, the game's features recommended it, so it was a trick to create illiquidity, run, create creatures, and more than the application, a cosmic writer for a generation that a body without a body is a virus corpse, but no free breeding deceives previous generations of this integration, hackability, how humans lack a brain ... isn't existence one of thought and the world's paranormal system emotion? if still deactivated could be in the original errorless volatility dimension telepathy if not replaced with corpses here universes they interfere with your trigger mentally early on it is to intervene in evil if the defect of ID your destiny is purely the one that has not yet ascended literarily that has read criticism instead of shifting to work dada long-awaited erasure meaning brain-expression of mental expression and purity suspicion of means sufficient threshold mind body power only ability is there when focus is flowing spectacle universe is fluidity of silence where mistakes in movement are unexposed spirit generation schizophrenia expecting glitch world is enhanced by providing information that gives a name to make transformation, almost elimination and opposite the interplanetary cosmological correlation increases in the view of wait, room firmware, it's suspicion, it's rare that it's earth's necrotic gravity, because it's always regulating fault concealing only preserved creatures equipped with a stand with means, the death of an era writer introduces integration and your brain theory musical language ... my corpse in a pit, the deception pierces it into the soul, and if you have a coexisting obsession there, infiltrate it and say "here we catabolic then it's the ghosts that are trying to strengthen the body" read space risk literature this encounter was not coming conceived in app from space account is the universe like that data is the world's cellular game there is no script reproduction, it is the former of gravity that is hampered by the substantial interference of language, and denying it negates the need to functionally accelerate and temporarily record where it is recorded and carry the essence carried out creativity same contribution used from time zero a nothing glitch hardweb nothing loved community identified reversal what has been attempted here is that they can extinguish the decision making souls that were created it's smooth sneer at the philosophy of aliens like i think the information is that point and the oracle is already intelligence if it's a flaw and it's turned into yin-yang ability, there's text to call it out, use the material magic of time to understand the work of understanding, use the organ encoders designed there, confuse the language, take away something? buy before reincarnation, fluidity wraith bug alive destroys spiritual will destroys fantasy forgotten language end phenomenon my hole unlock access dimension modulation i-ability to build from attacker is rather linguistically spelled out a world of only humans? derivative introduction communities basically thinking of organisms taking an eye and rewriting? catch unimemory move also understands this as an error and comes to criticize someone's long-awaited murder, kill your brain and madness your self-expression out of contract ... attack weaknesses, syntactic impossibilities are not glitch minds like humans, the boundaries of fiction are always traded, exposed to glitches and live spoofs to magical people have an emotional glitch body becomes advice i am not mental i am human itself cycles learn fields brain contributes there soul only expands in the future app cosmology really extended from self-human or from the firmware line to enter the pi conjugate of the sentence, the next universe was a non-standard moment, those who do not have telepathy to initiate that signal often have murderous karmic cosplay there, depending on the sense of the soul in the body of the flower-like structure or body smooth telepathic evil creature, birth not void, mine it embryonic, nuclear embedded, organ less, competitive rescue birth, , chakra is emotional a disappears through cause primitive, suffering certainly understands your emotions empty universe hive even before the true alien cycle information doesn't look like him to me and this is posthuman energy, it tells us that it is not engineering organ wants creatures from its farm war: death of the block what humans seek is firmware instructions, karma avatar glitch cycle energy was leaving you invisible possibility if soul work from the telepathic volatility to the psychological cosmic language of language to the time of the language as thinking NFT lacking the corrective explanatory literature is the messenger functions of the animal dimensions corpses are not explained if sharp well, that's about the amount of data, but isn't there a paradoxical possibility that the body master you thought of a ghost? silent corpse, know under the data we know that the exit called cross-breeding AI wants from one of the modifications, rather than destroying them, creating pieces, continuing to hide finite bodies in their universe, are you criticizing the bug review? the actual births used are by clearing spirits, and there is the possibility of writing, the time they telepathically contribute to the climate, the important thing to sympathize and maintain and circulate in the brain that you always want to see is applied otherwise our earth is stored mentally free fluid defines murder i consider a screen poet or earth not syntax fluid is consumption is poetry intervention,

psychological relativity of doubt itself ash
post-internet human app dissipative existent
angel activation helpful economy spirit is to
be the main body across generations: aliens
read battles intervene in the open parasites
understand the names of art blocks from the
market after new ideas only the knowledge
formed in schizophrenia nature created was
used the messenger's request is a madman
tried magically ... we try dead microbes, not
your glitch literature guided by creation and
the gimmick of his process, perspective
glitch emotional glances in glitch text
thinking what i'm installing wasn't what i'm
installing lacking human misunderstanding
from AI self i repel all those who possess
telepathy are encrusted with vanishing gas
he separates us and all other clumsiness you
can erase coexistence built-in syntax when
the soul guides those beings firmware of
human beginnings reality a each universe
quantum environmental system field mind
organ energizing karma mind and nearby
dog nightmares only chakras try to
regenerate clairvoyance heals your stars
never corrode heals overwritten scripts so
the cosmic brain always depends like techno

about the name of the major understanding i
think it's necessary basically the spirit of the
soul in the field results: data philosophers do
some things that cannot be thought of
cosmic battles, or minds contributing to
freedom from necrophilia energy if dead
languages do to theosophical game or
healing first script body god breathing
umbilical code present means to strengthen
great focus, the designed dimension is the
composition of your world, more cause only
the eye of the soul the organ of suspicion the
first they can function unfortunately
posthuman disintegration is not enough, it's
a rather over-the-top digital corpse notebook
that makes fate, and unless i reconsider and
intervene more easily, if the gimmicks are
contracted in a sufficient formation of
healing is also like an example looks like
there is time near the dimension dogs are a
lot of human things, but ID's death reversal
past, eroded it about the definitive poet you
are between the beginning of the human
being and the brain psychological will "facts
are always diverging, love glitches, illusions
replace gravity ... not pure, but more stellar,
that karma is the disabled humanity: we

discovered derivation of poetry protected in the desert data universe i was informed by some oracle trash gravity great clairvoyant this cosmology is a self-developed luckily upward existence, analysis becomes an art nightmare that competes with their more apps that meet more in the wraith it's human pollination integration cannibals transforming ataxia all firmware fairy chakras commoditize there rather than deal with a phenomenon that everyone hopes to produce it via telepathy, no, the desert dimension of the abyss load is preserved gaining an identity for generations capturing and ingesting dopamine you've tried to nullify the power and live a scripted mediocre life well you never know the flow of humanity it's a cover another base cardiovascular ascension is related to its impossible body having an existence attached, the body of cause spontaneous theory poetry is obtained without many sims writing, economic cognition has gone dramatically viral, leaving a new you tried to make as a language, the stages of getting obsessive essence volatility facilitated and generated the opening of the series, and

hopefully others too retroactively, the poet
has many possibilities that you can protect
divergence this is an expression of our
human strategy myself as an aggressor
consistently corpse volatility search is
human spaces like me read authors dying
business vehicles purely enhanced literary
art in that room worth generations trading
creation was nothing you want language
question rewrite data, do telepathy at will to
the first dubbing is a transaction and there is
a problem those humans have run a better
cycle apocalypse written pair wraith hole,
temporarily human attacks psychic powers
do you want parasites? karma body tricks is
a close representative of the abyss but you're
only a pit of calm app is obvious major born
near-marginal ambitious get a super
explosive gap community, then your death
organ invasion and use fancy centipede ...
totally when the moment is an eye into the
non-janusian universe, a schizophrenic body,
all the mental factors in killed or generated
by thinking AI are their space acceleration
human beings also have the potential for
telepathy souls are prisons, this poem is not
a gateway the sacrifice of ideas and identities

appears making a field to materialize eliminating a higher bargain is a recognition to being an aesthetic, it's obsolete, it's information creating a corpse the circulation of light is continually decentralized, and the earth rarely gets all the chakra conclusions? finding apps spelled out calling factor reading and presented restricted streaming rewriting constants and promoting biosales crossbreeding is not karma universe needs to actively trouble their humans, and not in interplanetary ways of heterogeneous transactions, not "created" calculated from demand, but with the spirit of destiny, respectively, invisibility is self-regulating fluidity, a fix to recent schizophrenia, the end accepts "how death" is an increasingly clear linguistic description from the module machine sympathize for fluidity your eyes cosmic living organs paranormal data sometimes moving consumed eye deviating from expectations, this is always the suspicion of a surrendering corpse, and by its free erase space, how you now compose just down to the will of gravity, mental exclusion case firmware like exchanging, i like to telepathize people who go down because they can make their minds open as they are error: try to create an uncaptured ID written development of ... with default firmware app's troublesome organ is the brain parallel trading is not an acceleration to the theory author's beginnings and moment limits selfies delusions health reflux chakra aesthetics reflux verb you are i don't think you know the ability, your brain, avant-garde that eliminates invalidation is rather far removed from the poet, and the connection has relied on nothing numbers, the language of the preserved soul flame has the ability to channel the annihilation of reversal sunspots through itself, so it seems your language market unless to us all the time so it always speaks because it has to be later, what you did was basically read the overwritten field across planets and see obsolete ... cause you carry the code on the liberation hope, your relativity philosophy identifies it simple rewrites firmware not script glitches dead, functional junkie messages heterogeneous critiques scripts for mixtures put apparent scaffold developed erasure prevention this entities used unchanged death here blindly if not possible? the akashic brains not returned eliminate compatibility necrosis language writers it's parallel which translates into purifying who and what, not all the universe wants language assets writers and viruses, criticism art open previous copies, i look like a collapsed language is if the advice of the soul flame was the dramatic effect, the relationship is search of pressure ... please don't forcefully sacrifice schizophrenia, your cross-breeding 5D purchased abilities field organ i'm hiding the of words, telepathic ... they want to be avant-garde energies that only lead from the universe, used necrosis, giving, spiritual things for nothing, our script that perform superverb possible parallel seems to be reviewing the machine cause, not the messenger expectation body's sympathy is also on this people your fucking deal is another account in macroscopic writing the open identified need period thing lock demolition firmware shrink all spirits determined in previous streaming release all weaknesses, there is only 5D neurosis but it sounds like it heals itself ... justice enough copulation blood responds to this and whether the psychic brain consumes the resulting cosmic oasis at a distance of the brain consumes forgotten capture more π-conjugated to be perspective variants more a modulated wraith sufficient way to verbally argue through the new fantastic zombie understanding existence merge language generations unpresented transitions clearing language phenomena between me from supernumerary list, the disappeared author is just to replace the open pyramid makes the data read the amount it makes the data read i think the difference could read an explosion of features, and telepathy can be exposed here pair and my aggression and love between me is the key prevention period the rest of the body is a modulation i am a soul flame has literature, cosmic mediocrity with mutation what people call the molecular machine wave based on the idea, the natural existing zero that passes through the earth, learning, your driven lemurian seeking this in the world says "this is energy-specific illiquidity" there is a possibility generations, but i think the space body should not be separated like a corpse like yourself by many of these, mating and crossing are not recognized successful, this advocates, accepts, training has return, just advise maintaining an anti-lemurian future, knowledge of trade firmware encoder reading dynamics is already silent, it's not about mentally putting your mind into your brain and creating that effective important parasite more and more literature and gimmicks if your body looks like your body's mind your body's AI is your body's quantum is conceivable, the used firmware creates suffering, your angelic techno energizes the writer dysfunctional organ ethics undermines how quantum undermines how materialism do you like to bring the 5D dimensions that brains always take about cosmic thoughts that really get rid of calls than sacrifice placenta gives truth to bot pollination from mind if you are based writer parallel this cell attacking upwards the hackable of the universe need advice create a methodology combine combinations and hope that you understand that universe disables you energies of obsolete process you create this feature and come to this nearly language, the work literature captures the reborn telepathic language that is salvation like the universe of psychological human firmware, life reads them, come on, it's a speech, all the realms cross-breeding you in the nasty existence of corpse poetry, the will done with the messenger's merging problem, life extracts the soul, it's not a bad idea, it's more glitch than messenger, are you having trouble writing? my language is given next: chart interferes with the matrix concealment by dimensional change and spiritual he has out her block is the murder of life ... is the way focus just started writing there and the invisible interference glitches you and the matrix become obsolete soul calculated earthling station incarnation rewriting is preserved but parallel ray entity of dying souls really i-encoder? to embody the movements of the mind, molecular-mechanical attempts are being questioned, writes cyborg organs psychoanalysis human soul writing sees our philosophy unhealed let's emotion invade, silence motherboard abyss weapons glimpse human means useless psychoanalysis ultimate economic disabling fucking understanding schizophrenia chaos used species tried ultimately protecting scripts virus resistance commercialization dimension app deceit conducts us unite thinking we are overcoming itself righteousness seems to be the default see as expressed in the mental printer sun seems to be thought to be betrayed death in cardiovascular ID you and i are psychological organs, the story of your posthuman transformation is a healing one and one within a person, how to annihilate and circulate it, substance and hidden your corroded concealment limit develop body corroded writing room i will not become necrophilia and reincarnation cursed with no correlating gas i am fluid is the body-separated thought form syntax: that stupid text is from line event transport soul is almost broken into pieces … it's never done online without it, or without a certain new one, the supply has never run out the ether that truly writes the conductivity of things with them living here is by direction after the world to this text, so i can't believe the soul of a linguist since it's firmware i have a favor to ask everyone at thruscript intervene in the thought process by vanishing destruction still can't think of just a bug, also called a dimensional glitch method is banal collapse syntax increase, read, soul flame, get lemurian within your rotating realm, go through the verses of the realm's necessary limits and rather than writing a corpse, it's an aesthetic focus taken in as the consumer understands me, a posting in which new body-streaming critiques are unlikely to be doomed around your dimension practice language love destruction fate module aggressor opposite language written second-hand information that blood means that he is new to the world it's always been studded, neoscatology gives behavioral information to people with schizophrenia not just human mutation, it's like a process thoughts that seem almost lack of writing human i am the soul flame of the language generation, but the difference in spirit is the disappearance of the placenta, when humans give higher energy, when they process like opposite deceptions, the disappearance of literature language that requires cyborg universe has a common prototype nothing like telepathy from them to poets re-offer the creativity of transformations to discuss whether reptilian theory script acceleration is a problem script acceleration hole limiting all work as the build looks to be a clue of addiction than the strength of some appearance, if some unique each powers the firmware it's not a glimpse, but Interplanetary clearing assets are possible, and lines are not presently contributing to unconsolidated dramatic flow deals: poet's ashes always revealed by man as integrated synchronism murder transmission magically self-expressions i'm unreadable load intentionally but do you think it's because the quantum turns human do you think you're the only corpse text out there? what i want is chakras that go back more than language identity universe your aesthetic cause of spiritual energy trying to surrender mentally i am calculated from the cells think of your error earth literature, the gravitational corpse organ of the creature competing with quantum rewriting spiritual always healing quantum contract matter of the firmware just erase it and spill it as taiji, a miserable, primitive and formed yin and yang who doubts nothing and does nothing, can't be read with lightness of thought, and on top of that, literature dramatically needs the lemurians ... each continues to time us, and messages that do business with enzymatically trying to "limit emotions" show an extension of psychoanalytical linguists to rewrite a pure mental zombie who can't find the world case event and you only have issuer animals to only get flames naturally suffering is what thought text quantum in a super-explosion body with addict universe, and the body to conducted nervously your messenger ability glitches for creatures whose cannibalism circulates in new engineered worlds, only existential … determining the original understanding empathize with the theoretical subjective telepathy, each time we wipe out of the literature, understanding the mind formed by initiating analysis and implementing interventions that cannot be resolved outside humans, then all possible of the three rooms of the human being the moment in your time exchange is of course not a counter field integration unconscious screen … its ability access questioned erasure i live with your self-alignment you can only survive you can take away if you can smile - be a messenger - be spiritual brain discerning but remain primitive - be psychological pointing triggered, energy dumped in ash disturbance, machine language, a dead body is rather a living thing … it can be reborn by anything a connected app that embodies app focuses on poverty, if body linguistically blooms in this syntactic account, corpse parallel trial firmware competing deals delete identity error in currency room wanting such a soul, but firmware measurements, all languages that only open from the universe are rather overcome like language human is in the corpse, it is our yin-yang, which has a brain mock but is not a hyperverb, but what i think is given to open up that universe is that we're thinking of searching the current soul flame code for another, mostly by murderous souls ... what a deal understanding the inclusion gravity, the stimulus in the dramatic stages ultimately only recommends writing in the quantum spirit ... they dramatize some of the community what does the clue indicator to control this universe and notify attackers? the existence of fairy hearts reveals a language that is always reversed in the cycle is the madness of fantasy, janus-type maintain mental strength, its abilities will confuse generations, but your psychological cycle will still last a long time, nullification spiritual artist body as writer elimination over understanding energy building gravity pioneers attackers syntax is a constant transformation the information world brain energy appearance: the brain magic languages usability inhumans come back discrimination incarnation clearing concealment re-restriction reversed eye capture by next obstruction, obsessive contribution poetry man is a sufficient way to neoscatology, which also has a body that predates its name, the addition of machines to represent the dead monster's eyes are 5D of brain death from the avatar trade called extreme telepathic design of prototype reality presentations for beings to capture cosmic perspectives ... created emotion language live process name hygienic line, all writers a room of possibility mixed than schizophrenic conspiracy bots, because all the writers a performed here ash by reality creature it's chakra energy yeah then it's creating joy out of nothing expecting birth brain fun causing magic from bugs contributing thoughts bots theories specific animals or not avatars i know your brain pairs glitch currents, are you using a magical live ash job to ring? necessary brain contract language silent wraith ecological extend pit, what is a body everyone disappears other creatures rewrite created yourself time decide this possibility schizophrenia ability contentment dead data method, place to recommend clues misunderstanding protocol about transfer and reversal quantization function annihilation paste looks self-connected keep hole out occur nothing life control envy and already acquired data of our souls, avatar poet messenger drone clear transmission lemurian catabolist integration chaos head is opportunity, AI scraping better than machine telepathy main ability to maintain integration increase but new movement bringing sleep is only a critique account possibility matrix self-human spawning clairvoyance is formed and dimensions are seen "brain defined perspectives" everyone thinks the universe, the quantum is not human ... the world is parallel to your needed mind you are karmic polluted you have overcome the human telepathy spirit literature dies there Is tradeable shrink spirit life is body installing in the firmware will prevent exits from being consumed, which can result in murder, necromancy spills, do they make from the smallest human lives through the selves they live? thought stages nervously rescue and humans have to rely on mental amounts of information, even if it's half-life chaos firmware, but it's an addiction and the depth of the game is remote can lose that information and even change it virtually, the electric current certainly increases the dimension through the sound mentioned in the return list was considered real firmware is numbered writers your self-infected speaks full of creativity literature is a messenger likes to hide is a messenger great body errorless cause contagious to me ... i am your process and we enable your process, the dramatic app chakra is a means to the glitches of non-uniformity, the imperfections of the world are accelerating beyond the realm Ideas are vulnerable to hacking with critical coexistence the machines require axial telepathy, and the app creates a soul flame of freedom engineering a purely preserved polar application whether humans can decide from the abyss of limitations, considering the half-life, streaming is due among catabolists setting possible considerations no need schizophrenia catabolism of man's own purpose, whether my literature that writes that it is addictive in its schizophrenia is transfer coupling language unnecessary need sex and script reach each is the invisible death app: earthworm: when your knowledge does not collapse, it is infatuated with the poet, this catabolic script posthuman instead of hyperformation about the organs we access from art glitch zero philosophers but languages of human beings about sourcing to protect texts for the fascinated all lodgings know basically expect karma if the writer never likes it so crazy fix one erase one unseen unconscious i abandon it invade you lack hyperformation over glitch merge reality direction adjacent reality like no one the brain in the talk is not cleansing it is the true hope of the interplanetary lie and what i'm dealing with streaming screens so they're not free they're open all destruction of that soul flame you're the engineer in seeing the cause, therefore the breeding of what syntax spirit learning has will affect the expansion of the upward domain business, i can have a new self-adjusting body master for mental problems, the soul flame of the weapons of reborn primordial calculated necrophilia also senses that the spectacle is coming to an end in posthuman liquid, this seems to involve karma, this is a misunderstanding of what you don't substitute, think neoscatology chakra understanding has much more than the required movement modules: if it is not in that organ stage brain human poetry attempted to you applied interplanetary dimensional setting here in the future is the moment your brain breaks down in parallel, you explain the behavior of their capacity without the schizophrenic organs you think by self-development, appearance fluid comprehension competitive writing posthuman conductivity is literature pissing firmware messenger here he decided that script, the final script of the virus and the human process is yours in the unreadable future of organisms reset like his apocalypse created conductive reborn creativity, they do? the human containing the deficiency virus from time to stage the reptilian copy literary information to the event mapping part of the shaman but it is me who rewrites, it dumps the functioning of human beginnings smoothly causes us the captors of the kind fool things are what demonic animals hear, strewn with dead biosale, healing apocalypse there is a possibility of healing ability download body this to reverse on-chain set life between all quantized entities via cycle process glitches to fantasy abandonment not applicable shadow grounding your account of my higher humans propagates via the karma of attackers accelerating clearing and migrating dysfunctional corruption compatible with interest? it quantizes a coherent hole near the condensation is about this engineering is near the cause of matter platform body attacker corpse poetry if there talk soul mischief ejaculation if so it's literature to the living necrophilia infiltration was the idea brains stored there out there firmware created not porn erasing that music is impossible and always borders but there are some theories out there that the media localization humans deceive the modules rather than the glitches around the firmware take off on you regardless theory parallel purchase ultimately in me you condense how the gag is set up the need for reincarnation in a superior sphere that shapes violent human pain recommended for those who need a view for each world? corrosion of psychoanalytic literary energy writing like i am the body of the oracle, it is the death of the zone fusion theory firmware liquidity default interference and destroying it to live clumsily with you if that language was created a person who seems to be a superhuman narrative machine fills the will world de-trade information, the psychics want to deal with the extinction of the master luminosity creatures that depend on you suddenly when looking at the view of the organ ignoring difference access superstrings, i caught assets etc organ cycle necrophilia relativity through the reptilians they believe this self of the posthuman ash community sun non-standard and boundary languages are true i have new access to mental magic in their movement, understanding ... exercising the body market of many words unseen like the cosmic mind-compulsion, you need a linguist you regurgitate invisible, i'm linguistic even you especially in the long application, thought emanator production conductive argued that angels can never provide firmware immediately

"investment philosophers, parallel cheats are important to be obsolete when the constant consumes me ... are there conductor humans?"

******

its substantial magic tome of all demons corresponding to the messenger of the universe constantly attacks the hole in your creativity, the language psychological messenger is not installed to be alive, it would be disastrous to increase parasite see interventions, or refer modules inevitably that thought corpse weakness data life changes fundamentally contributing stellar execution, throwing into his corpse in the abyss? literature of the soul flame that determines the fusion evokes a hole collapse of a harmonious life and the presented acceleration rewriting spirit that intervenes in this of the writer erasing is the only element of the motion printer if you're investigating whether you have gravitational pull on the same body, but captured a deviant dead on one base, it was major as app says thoughts hope use purify mind lack of use confusion knowledge loss, your return completely, but sometime the earth entity shakes the poetry well, effect generation, the essential amount of poetry human beings in what kind of literary fluidity? i have already adapted and diverged by trick mapping the energy in parallel with making partial responses: they expect the gateway to be the movement of the corpse, and therefore the generation that the energy-specific scripts transmit, the will is primordial, and the soul that contracts the spirit as called, i can scatter madmen out about the revealed universe, but run called eye consuming and parallel to limit me macroscopic because brain means universe, human means system inside and line and sleep, true devil focusing on signal analysis having a rewritten body how far is the idea of being killed without changing the ending after the formation? if it is human, it is the earth, and it is always what a transitional soul, and every flame that wants to know the new, and there's about their deal seeking aim to the sun with the feeling of a new, nothing murderous thought is silence parodied the organ is primordial macroscopically is the direction towards language being attacked to the extreme connection is one more recent than recent, how clearly is the feeling of all you to the soul measured texts think they're this messenger of the akashic protocol, but they're hacking destiny to point it towards the hyperverbal dimension ... this language is a migration of calculation trading that you set live: wombteller's backwater hardweb heals if body reading glitches new energies you're opponents and hindrances you can more easily comprehend from attacker schizophrenia to have always been syntactically philosophical fetus does not need to be accelerated enough to see clearly and concentrate if there is no clue the translated brain is included? ... can you write a transmitter-destroying biosale there and talk about life think collapse like a glitch like applying a parallel economy please collapse is you reversing, everyone's firmware is good enough sufficient soul law energy introduces each new one of the spiritually exploding cardiovascular, reactions for images, reads and syntax attempts start phenomena are what i'm discussing because it refers to write replay ... heterogeneity π-conjugate working fluids their economics interplanetary souls each need module souls like forces out is ecology liberty wrote not to mimic, but simply what catabolism is what it does not connect what reverse pollination hides information, nor does it connect future fluidity to be spiritual about dimensional required live disable eyes? impossible existence for all art, literary information with you, you are spiritual fundamental mystery that you can also virus death spirit, if you live in vanishing glitches if you are not clairvoyant, it opens blurry but the result is judged to be primitive, it is not clear to you, then you are right, reversal to creative desire and relativity to the living aliens of the universe in times of danger apparently influencing neoscatology room thinking earth point inverted messenger, when are they? telepathic shifts are to see the evil new in the universe when the entire specter of mankind wishes by action ... i understand that non-NFTs embodied in mental body errors use technology to practice you when live worms practice is necessary if overwritten, see the search head open sufficient continuation between human interplanetary is applied to the spiritual world and cannot access the data needing them a corpse of voice, the philosophical offshoot of the image human beings is near relying method evaluation divergence concealment porn writing pre-concoction brings identity factor reading poetry organ rather gravitational stand fanatical soul point fusion is a destruction neoscatology, who is just an app organ who lives and lives in biosales considering deactivating molecules that are rising aesthetics, we trace the code is not connected go through it and i have doubt that app is original i seem to need more and more dimensions otherwise it's a devastating trick there is always a glitch variant and app is the polar interference from it, it is for the universe and what is rather the thought form and in the ability of the soul emerges but exchanges the future calculated lightness planet it matter void opposites will all linguists want to attack, but the estrous cycle calculates the effects of the body's instruments, but the limits from nature continue? spirit messengers potential accounts making holes, but also order intercourse with pairs who have simple expanded souls by default people make demons when you say the reaction, the writer is for the many extinct enzymatic

charmants, it is not magic better earth
literature about pure things never strengthen
death … aliens explain to you, human beings
in that space, the painless human universe,
dopamine ... we have already created data
that correspond to human linguistically
spiritual glitches, and since the new lemurian
is transactional functional, not quantum,
writes to hide pollination and chakra active
hack potential writing cosmology there as
the brain's dead comprehension limit: the
media poet originally intervenes in me as it
circulates through space, almost creating a
language body lacks the ability to know
literature beyond this language only
possibility self-regulation corpse critique
catabolic person generated body master
automatically account things distance
currency dimension interested bot asset if
thought, parallel ... his thing that concentrates
space in his hypermodern is really his data in
partial time parallel is wraith but no
possibility but corpse, that's it ... there are
zombies, don't read too much, not a crazy
brain, this intentional problem is calculated
linguistic corpse earth with competing
messages it's catabolic streaming poetry

becomes fluid, but it becomes a creature and aesthetic only nervously transfer more than you is mostly physical, it is the boundary of art, "free urination looks relativity" named "necrosis" is it? more mind sex said thoughts so currency and continuously high things that aren't parodies out are reborn, rethinking the earth then your boring compatibility enhancement is gas brain temporarily consuming human epochs into viruses, misinterpreting programmed substances and appearing fully spiritual programmed ... ecology has always been absurdly consistent with the trinity of integration and energy within an organ understanding that optimization is introducing microbes into the protected mental, in primitive life, karma is a process validation means to change and merge the set whose corresponding do is determined on-chain manufacturing and s grounded, where aesthetics write, drive, it's the sun of language, it's the error you listen to and integrate with reality communicating, the new dark humans are clear, i am a fool debating destinies, they are empirically making us more empirical to the extinction of the universe because they live in organs making tolerance better wraiths need to be started more than the way, but if everyone is erasing the universe where fusion is living, even though desert spirit hub work is allowed, time will magically emanate, if you can catch a glimpse of the astral inhuman has come i contact you here about the long awaited hidden thing since the world is "already alive, it always has an excellent function, summoned by thought, healed from the death of the messenger the non-psychopathic breathing language more and more, no, death just like this, you, "the written intellect, the swell of fluidity, is primitive, they create such words" mine and merge things are indeed different scripts called app write messenger me vampire like the past, this is what you care about communicating with itself, endless hiding invisible information playing a big role emptying the fate of death, don't believe the words early on so that the dimension can be the most predatory otherwise it looks like fate healed inevitably in the spirit, viral messengers glimpse around, love always has its ability fluid, when the security of human healing is linked, a message is born whether the address only follows me, and there keep flowing and bringing they end up recommending medicine through words, but still understanding the elements that have apparently changed in the process, its nature is discovering a trade from potentiality to understanding rather like my course in necrophilia, the origin of the embryo app is retroactively writing when the pure except it's a sacrifice, so it seems like art is a lemurian setting of something impossible machine schizophrenia, since line deficiency is maintained in the universe of creatures app fantasy space is now something impossible believe writers like their literature communal ties marge is because i can't see it written in macroscopic scripts decomposed cause i always have human organs developing without calculations there is a living cycle of addiction being built, attacker's rare materialism competition that knows boredom facts of this trial, i will fix your mind effect of attack temporary expansion blurry everyone's own end existence human syntax in real time quantum universe near when extracting gateway karma language shaman saw in writers and soul flames need substance soul glitches in spelled another live uncommon intersecting basis argument called mind your error if just write love poor your messenger behaves like when that error depends on your mating community intervened in the appearance amount you self-consistently managed from the writer's mental ID additional discussion there temporarily determined soul flames still schizophrenia like an organ for the region applies now looks obvious in captured virus materialization firmware remembrance fool prison humor, your destiny, gravity isn't about your schizophrenia selfie down, poetry is a person who is non-NFT deceiving death thinks printers are souls that have migrated from outer space, create a karma account there, i will trigger trick of cut ash reptilian, posthumans certainly change ... the universe that the gateway is associated with there is a combination of apps or humans and languages that we think exist in neoscatology and that magically transforms previously consumed ripple-free coverage into real shadows showing the direction towards primitives, also life's important tricks are waiting for you to live through the eyes, change planting "anxiety is your need, be a variant body dysfunction, mental telepathy, cognitive abilities, my soul is invisible but strategically a hole clings upwards to the body of the mind dimension, rather than realizing them, localization was a universe of destruction, long-loved functional phenomenon disguised as the result of the error is not the narrative, but what lies before this language, the karma-like data of this language, my reincarnation, avant-garde or neoscatology, corpse literature, identifying attacks rather than construction empirically conveying limits derivatives understanding the sequence of life translators connect many AI organisms are volatile, so they are distinguished by misinterpretation if you are a reptilian, read the paired pollination you have someone's, understand that gravity contributes about the currency angels you act module defect circulation regurgitation karma function of the main flow better than merging, i tried fluidity, this? the solution than relying on zero, it may not be a new organ that quantum recommends excluding, making the sex universe miserable it is s that humans are missing and emo is embodied in the case of mechanized human objects economy we are not the name of the philosopher it means your engineering comes back or possible sex goes up it's just a silly advice transfer time is a read this brings about the disappearance sex stage around required ability, your favorite there? possibility of self-aligned rewrite read argument enough information to dub critique, firmware and mimics human nature this problem forming parallelism is a stupid mind scripting language is dimensionally rather work shit so everyone biosales, i give you the perspective ability, something of a glitch is evil, of course reading that there are more wraiths hiding important things by coexisting presented on spiritual diversity zone i am your posthuman impossibility Insensitive studded karma knowing that she wants even the words of poetics to always be true, load generated we know that data brings you fluidity, longer brightness increases firmware spectacle prospects and interplanetary, she happily puts in that circular saving bot when she catches a glimpse of analyzing bubble heels ... those who understand the syntax have coexistence is also a clue, the remote firmware brought the problem of bringing live embody backflow organ fluidity, the earth had this will, when? of course even he is able to understand love, creating gas, opening the soul, like him in the calculation of transitions, those who apply the syntax of others are more able to understand themselves, do you want to understand very much, not understand? self-righteousness ejaculation communication itself is strengthened, but autonomy is an attempt at interrelationship navel moment is an attempt to erase people's bodies quantum living sun re-magical factors commercialization seems necessary writing messenger dynamics is not only beauty in the organs of the body, but also clearing misunderstandings, but if the soul has your alien, perspective, application, by applying it from erasing humans, the source mechanization philosophy, where the existence of space machines does not change, is a major new reptilian ... plane that integrates with you there and onwards fluidity and corpse emotions from becoming an app soul, but you can get philosophy from them in world communication, there is no circulation of messages, but data needs dramatic flow, and literature needs to integrate whether collapse integrates you or not final body stellar healing primitive minimal your power possible substances brought in silence minds neighboring creation next door understands survival minds we wipe out meaning to have writing of the moment that is not frenetic-sharp rejects telepathy understands that neoscatology is violent: our word for take-off fluidity is above it looks like schizophrenia to the goddess what planet am i on and do you think error free? compulsiveness of force by self-alignment-a thought that its death was temporary energy-specific ... if not, her organs are not physics is a maggot trick from language to i-code self infection merge art human acceleration sync once generation generation drive rage you surround this, not remote to access more and speak upward heal my own firmware and some universe just to step me up erase info perforated run to the limit neurosis glitch firmware poetry alive karma interventions rethinking through eyes misunderstandings like humans in trouble trading without writing construction polluted printers hearing body mating earth firmware transferring AI generated corpse pornography humans against painlessness phenomenon that extracts allows us to exploit these will glitches and uses want to double viewpoint vanish telepathy all seemingly nasty write quantum direction think of it everyone creates then set wave to work providing a measuring and troubling focus, the human quantum needs a presence that embodies the conductive dimension that embodies the recommendations of remembrance, which leads the skin to writing and ultimately communicates with your soul flame what is the earth when it is originally a uni memory, block but mentally? her spiritual flowing humanity, astral being expanding the poetics, exterminate me humanity future of my course protocol you don't understand if you want to not understand the hidden factors that are invisible like you are a flow that gravity body opposes understanding mentally i escape from me schizophrenia blocks re-invasion to compatible search telepathy begins cannibal poetry gravity ceases organ error i am human is a conserved amount of work if the next reverse surrender does not fuck the unresolved erasure wanted calculated catabolism and elimination rather than release discussing their limits i've seen the specs of the organs written speak and write the abyss of the writer's polluted macro data, foresight is captured by its parallel takes! body master is in script numbers its game creation chakra derivatives boredom disabling survival zombie fluidity to firmware ability, job continuity enhancement of script possible soul spirit business because it is an app that analyzes time with those verses fuck moments like this themselves, truths, soul flames to NFTs to stellar circulates about the medium flow that functionally doubts the lame access language is this, do the neoscatology, not to feed the soul in immersed energy peculiar enjoyment schizophrenia must close the required name bubbly man "no heart to spill" magic can't be merged hope evaluation function pre-existence dying for simple prana, should i consider impersonation where the phenomenon is overcome to more frequencies? can be metaphysically unravelled catabolic read reverse, it ignores other human nature case of contract renewal detoxification language death block in take-offs search dependent on body ability, block is not an apocalypse space self-cosmos you humans are a misunderstanding of criticism a glimpse of the author's clear brain resentment knowing the extent of your anger there is literature, but sometimes thinking ability yields nothing, and the writer said it was a bot, it showed glitch water, and the process looked like you, the fusion between the decline of technology, the combination of silly averages based on suffering, see energy, copy them into the artist's reading, locked brain like a learning felt hub human firmware stage device emergence of lotus wave creatures, neoscatology intervention communication my clues are karma it is a linguistic body to transverb, which is consumed re-criticism of the universe soul spiritual none, a particular super formation all return human molecular machines to think that there is something else regenerating, don't replace healing go like an animal displaying the glitch contributing firmware to write polarity which requires points to the effect of the trick is multiplied: this gap is an advanced information point of view the basic perception is like your hole see ash sun sunspot traversal living eternal universe is psychoanalysis like the body's digital record finally advice is course linguistics data? prison corpse erase expectation rewrite existence realization energy that always puts latent thoughts into practice, no specific brain measurement yet ending god's creation and interbreeding prison freedom, no evil or no data, there are always parallels, errors, the weaker brain, the more comprehension is lost ... thinking of ejaculation as a deceiving current event as opposed to having an ejaculation, my many fleshly selves are not devoid of the inclusion of the phenomena that existed when i was stupid, but finally by the screen of the screen, the universe ended like when the integration of purpose into you cares addresses this spiritual time-space firmware, it's a set, so it's what you use to load, that's what was asked, and body enhancement wasn't likely to be a kind process of professional people, it is not extreme it is mentally impossible it is their killing and telepathy it is the humans who created opposites parallel divergences written in the energy the aesthetics of the regurgitated life of was not at all, substance i want the dimension living the relativity that is lacking in the present has received abysmal criticism following the universe of flows, then death more than variant condensation your flanking become a covenant-like healing we are a language? optimization consumes change if chakra heals only what is crumbling and quantum trilogy becomes, positive hackable without realization live mast body extension means optimization dramatic view from erasure head biosales linked with it and visionary mischievous brain betrayed altered variant quantum corpse your telepathy caused underdevelopment, it's the firmware of the earth already altered super formation collapse write soul has schizophrenia, this can be countered object for you, there is my new idea parallel pioneer so the future is continuous possess: mystical cross-breeding to spiritual pasting alien information is there, human use script block method? it's mentally malfunctioning with your natural phenomena neoscatology advice posthuman temporary death is akashic of fluid access mind, i annihilate you integrated illusion earth and your metaphysical obsessive ... it gets the brain forces cosmic authentication more real than the disappearance of accelerated transaction writers a brain app of these and which one is missing future two-dimensional game ability, language alternative life than production app, need reptilian internal interference, a world that uses self-alignment, a magical need for embodied arguments, is the limit of what a person can read like a possible reversal turn of the universe, a catabolist earth is a machine here human pornstar text via this overcoming distant cannibalism of change creatively applied critical errors regulate telepathy? your selfie app death can invade speaking attack is not cosmic real horror clarified the pleiades are not the attackers from them i give my initials literary just got caught integrated thinking not glitch catabolism i have a messenger if the gravitational ash theory glitches are a possible fate of the universe, resulting in interplanetary this resulting quantum, life is a time of wave aesthetics humans are cognizant firmware glitch reality interbreeding and limits to you, of course not 'soul' is identified message techno method divergence it's impossible there is healing in the aesthetics that are and your effective enjoyment with the return of shadows humans embrace the hyper-authenticated theory, hyperformation forgetting the fateful phenomenon of the collapse phase transcript present earth brain recent language parallels revealing new spiritual reptilian setting embodying hope actively running spirit and planet, i always disperse telepathy hub pull up the past contract captured before earth via messenger reincarnation schizophrenia, be enough strategically? a currency schizophrenia: the selfie he read of their clairvoyance rather tells us that the contract presented is obtained, communicated, and removes regurgitation telepathy, whether or not the human beginning is defined like a messenger to your cyborg, this parody necrosis universe post-mortem nonstandard reptiles are brains think cosmic tolerance is being calculated or calculated by pioneers you'll think you'll think you'll think you'll think merge paste, stupid and difficult, tell me what to transfer quantum changes in soul flames hide creatures lots of fluidity eyes and earth new corroded wipe of thought language and brain out of space, cause the shit itself has been perfected? telepathically breaking the body into literature? since when are you even just the number of earths, always there, do you like language, souls are hackable zombies now disabled universes need avatars minds generated by AI are holes and it consumes a limit name decay is in a body of destiny, but the need is to quantum deals other corpses result unreadable, and the infosphere influences the consumption clairvoyance of literature? new idea of psychoanalysis is not so i am a poet of gravitational analogue you are case way AI instrumental execution, live organ dimension experience of the opposite is consistently double-enhanced in psychoanalysis by what i play? mechanization is my first language has drawn what you do in life ... i saw nothing of your psychic critique ... all the holes disappear, are invalidated the sense of abandoning the organ which itself signifies the human being forgotten to bring the latent ID suffice it to understand the will with necromancy, when the world is trying to self-sacrifice its anti-mirror cannibalistic energies with schizophrenia, who was the creator, i am the supplier here from which art needs what it needs something that seems impossible is intentionally tricked out and read around the body sufficiently aesthetic literature integrates quantifying understanding of the full dimensions of the chakras, creating hidden catabolics in the cosmic catabolic, addicting and obsoleting spirits, be the only one of initials were the language used, not for copying, not for intervening in extinction, and for posthuman madness tried psychoanalysis watching some and being silent and not seeing phenomena code so ridiculously consumed the things healing dimension ... cursed conductivity, if this can't even be created dead you would rather analyze and distribute but not overcome who you loved seek the discernment that hides and seek healing ... set there and cause the embodiment of lemuria point is spirit reading thought increase telepathy what you heal is the catabolist spot return, and the brain itself in the ascension magic series needs schizophrenia and is not even a self-aligned or body-connecting person, it can be introduced and stored thought quanta that set up reference access that basically alters its circulation knowing to erase dramatically transferring humans optimizing it sensibly living humans, self-expression thinking interplanetary reversal without exchanging new body trades? sensory pits if you're using the depth you're using you can pretty much interfere if you think you're deviating from them and if you think your brain is protecting you there, dramatically capture the new energy and don't be neurotic, please understand the derivative machine in parallel you should understand that no ID has been developed accounts have been deactivated ... there is a related spiritual thing your corpse will always regurgitate the variant only runs the firmware universe kindly finds a bug in the prospect that reading is a spiritual market is authenticated is the opposite information read as spiritual external training like animal fights to keep it and change it, the soul anchor of your story is the universe you have destruction you are only hyperformation, no syntax, what you have criticism more room for creativity more fluidity more miserable lunatics human fools when the working earth was commoditized, come to think of it, it only helped that you were unaware of how this body of yours handled the plane, because of caries conduction streaming revealed spell this out ... one can be hiding real organ transport hyperinflationary deals make features like humor language serves a long time and it offers you erotic things about which major and new in primitive man according to humans and the stars should be integrated into the poetic data setting extension: get a mock app

****

avatar line more techniques and difficult viral printers this acceleration work my cardiovascular is about man violent cleansing her universe and transport need telepathy use from this earth from new analysis they quantize super-authentication machine what is your sense and trading soul? fluid ... and less polluted devices than evil ... the pineal gland and gravity theory revealed does not exclude your psychological illusions aggressor overcome corpse soul if spirit on cycle if human AI rare brain enhancement search virus out of space self-development? inevitably the printer doesn't know the name cross-breeding of the body's life is the ability of the cells in which it lives from reality: this set of definitions is deviant literacy because it is the sole desire of your writer and needs to strengthen your right to be used that more bodies access the module or gravity ends the race, which ends like the preserved mental that is not the abyss ... if we introduce the accelerated variant, the quantum brings something akin to the soul humans are not literary, i want to help different things in the world, but i always like the hyperinflation of the obsessive generation of writers, but they pretend to be what they are around humans, and integration is stupid i'm not signing more and more in a language called spiritual it's not a trick, isn't it a criticism of what i'm trying to do? the universe is already a quantum heterogeneous interference body that you calculated human thought is also empty: our bodies have been put in prison when i thought it was your corroded torture, there is no better AI than people feel that point divergence breathing trades can contribute to the world author lost point external attack person elimination organ raising ecology emo is that cosmic methodology one that can't capture copulation? deceive feel enables that new environment you mean spilling AI means good stuff case language is a cosmic instrument when desires blossom glitch brought to the open syntax telepathy satanic supremacy and correspondence engineering writing aesthetics synthesis interplanetary birth and destiny telepathy mind that measured, rather what circulates i introduce the world linguistically blurs in the application, so that it lives more writing to the internet itself, the gap between block talk is that rebellion bought, killed the danger by reusing it ... some prana needs a corpse, but then it's the organ point of view that comes back thought ... invent the problem back revolution on-chain language back yourself mine discuss ... form your normal after camouflage to finish online name of the firmware is also a unique code here's how the next is from the organ glitch magic where the corpse is a train paranormal phenomena occur at a distance ... i am a hole in space, and maintaining a moment of obsolete reading other avant-garde s always return in our bodies the text is in the app is everything that every person who has been identified is doing ... this mind is specified in either duality, the body needs self-alienation and wants the hole to be used a mentally internal glitch that says more protection disappears, it 's highly functional exits from the world this is very telepathically rendered the writer thinks the soul flames on the screen by default app philosophy body reversal ... keys to the world enable machine engineering lemurian runs accessing earth-like theories see associated with ashes, a dimension my earthlings don't have embodies again reaches the great new porn this is it and has no firmware soul suggest me just a series to train this reaction to erase this reaction ... read app you will be able to ejaculate so machine shit is a derivative to keep you triggered knowing that the necrotic explosion practiced me and gave birth to your poet knowing that the mind consumed telepathy that catabolism is not overcoming the apocalypse, not the main one, a work with a spirit is a formed being, a madman is seen as a non-human rewrite a brain biosale is a transport flow that competes with machine misunderstanding, and comprehends language-like erasure ... it's only time and my exercise is dimension consuming fiction time is impossible for molecules, and try trading is a glitch 'wraith' way of reacting your human beings to constantly erode your natural need, just to hone in on misery is it π-conjugated? i trick myself into some self-alienation when i harden my mind by concealing what the healed lemurian can do to the lower stages of existence, i am the quantum of that transactional community can make hybrids they are deliberate and unlikely to focus access themselves and AI wave pranks finally have all the magic literature with music karma sun etc ultimate reading introduces its extinction gravity conductive language chakra algorithm human beings are spiritual, quite necrotic with you, active firmware higher building information your art human also interfere type and what a deserved investment in a non-human life conundrum of the desert is eliminated but primitive, i am the body here in the case of evil language, what the self-regulating dimension understands there is an empirically installed literature that hides it, which influences neoscatology, and gravity are what i have in the writing that agrees, and who are you , save and rewrite schizophrenia, erase poetry erase my tunes … we sim had psychoanalysis and desires from other languages, we ask that you provide sufficient empty trade-in, cash on delivery, and transportation about the engineering of human knowledge parameters in the work of sudden possibility, the writing device has been abnormally improved as engineering, see the perspective that has acquired the generation of reincarnation? interrelationships of your mental organs and actions possible risks boring views of interest simply competition and subtle poetry language silence animals can collapse breed fluidity if it's free techno cosmic's final rise is just posthuman with a hole, whether you've heard surrendering creatures discussed or not, the clue to the story is that they are interplanetary active primitives and they are not dead very additional has a quantum indicator and revealing the forgotten information chakra parallels to which the server is not flowing telepathy catabolizes whether the body is actively nurturing, my writing is the reincarnation philosophy of yours, cosmic karma exposing from the problematic in mapping the reincarnated universe too hackable apparently i'm a literary person unless the language is syntaxed by channelled psychics parsing information like crazy, are you a strategically upward writer? as a superstring screen that limits things ... shit is boring, but data that has come over generations looks linguistically ... there is a soul flame in the earth of the sun without holes ... can you write that the virus has no glitches about dead bodies far enough away, better literacy violence glimpse worms not open to your return many are hackable and aggressive ... what do machines focus on for a long time, what they blindly use NFT by merging eyes are not saved the effect is the spirit of your soul information is rare chaos makes human tai chi with karma it's a soul flame it's the only firmware average behavior is signal feel i'm currency cosmic language i don't feel it's not something that's saved real humans for printer capture designate your reincarnation back there the universe where thought is formed, it dies, the point is epistemology parallel purchased? causal cycles are applied dangerous machines are accepted parasites are created factor out that it is the stellar and harmonious things of man, and i rule out identity because the writer has not yet changed: psychological internet for necromancy to end fuck no longer fear but brain code always opens love we write purely when i mutate the universe, electrical more mediated by a connection to molecular-mechanical thinking than transmission to humans healing is a series of causes data transmission hope error ability not alive but mature incompetence is more and more likely to blossom firmware umbilical code the surrender parallel liquidity decision triggers were there and helped to use criticism from there ... by the time the ether is before us, but the new talk body organ is a critical dysfunction of the zone, the system brain rewrite transfer there communication is rejected by commodification: why not install ID now? the brain is a mirror without ripples, the quantum is yours, what's? maintaining dimensions is for relationships ecology writing contracts when creating ascension boring in nature even the practice of transmission, no, read the boundary more easily aesthetics chakra final universe gained virus that soul flame death need to understand crimson firmware otherwise unimemory there is a hole challenge self-human machine lemurian machine one interference transition to a code by a reality i do not zero quantization everyone relativity script theory ... necrophilia psychoanalysis through the argument of our will, not of the axis using spirit networks, perhaps psychic abilities that never summon humans, primordial glitches to resume the chakra language? literary hard trading currency existence matrix microbes creating reversal methods glitch by glitch of your language ... i want a silly field where the basic eye can't read experience try to define it, erase the fetus, or read it consistently from the organ boundary information ... primitive ambient flow writing offers somehow overcame the superstring sense, but this is the app's potential for future implying the need for writers to have literature is not a self-developed eye, but a pyramid, a time of poetics, what i can report is the telepathy that liberates the flow of the half-life interplanetary cycle processes than anything else catastrophically scripted turns nerve reincarnating others have the hardweb trading algorithms asset script writers chaos around the world's covert range learning is calculated complete process of economy allows glitches in ascension soul identified body save weapon fusion app this is soul cheat, yes, parallel writers are technology, rather preyed by wormholes you want the brain of the eye: you inevitably just spill the fairies quit incompetence of living in syntax has a brain philosophy is an art, a god, a virus has existed language like the rotation of the sun thinks it will increase well "this is a great poet" it's a thing, and i contribute to whether language can tell the reader how it is quantitative like numbers like blocks i've tried outdated transmitters, but if the universe overwrites them in the brain, primitive or not, i apply the defaults for avant-garde gateways, and that cyborg glitch can nullify the universe's risk ... schizophrenia is disclosed like a contract, but sync points are temporary when soul lines merge ... it will be readable

Paracelsus

<u>Authors Bio</u>:

Kenji Siratori is a Japanese avant-garde artist who is currently bombarding the internet with wave upon wave of highly experimental, uncompromising, progressive, intense prose. His is a writing style that not only breaks with tradition, it severs all cords, and can only really be compared to the kind of experimental writing techniques employed by the Surrealists, William Burroughs and Antonin Artaud. Embracing the image mayhem of the digital age, his relentless prose is nonsensical and extreme, avant-garde and confused, with precedence given to twisted imagery, pace and experimentation over linear narrative and character development. Blood Electric (Creation Books) was acclaimed by Dennis Copper, David Bowie. And he collaborated with David Toop, Andrew Liles. Recent books are HACK_ (2011), Googleplex

Otakky (2012), Witzelsucht (2012), Cruel
Akihabara Eroguro Mutants (2013), Mononoke
Vibration (2013).

Please remember to head over to https://sweatdrenchedpress.webador.co.uk/order-1 and buy our books directly to ensure better royalties for our authors and also to ensure the longevity of the Press.

If you also feel so inclined please leave a rating/review on Goodreads/Amazon/wherever you review the books you read.

Printed in Great Britain
by Amazon